Striking a chord . . .

Mrs. Simmons looked a little confused at my abrupt farewell, but she didn't seem eager to change my mind about leaving. As soon as the door clicked shut behind me, I sprinted for Bess's car. I flung the door open and jumped inside.

"I was right," I said breathlessly. "I just saw something in there that confirms what I was thinking: Leslie Simmons has been kidnapped!"

NANCY DREW
girl detective™

Available from Aladdin Paperbacks

NANCY DREW
girl detective™

#3 **False Notes**

CAROLYN KEENE

Aladdin Paperbacks
New York   London   Toronto   Sydney

First Aladdin Paperbacks edition March 2004

Copyright © 2004 by Simon & Schuster, Inc.

ALADDIN PAPERBACKS
An imprint of Simon & Schuster Children's Publishing Division
1230 Avenue of the Americas New York, NY 10020

Manufactured in the United States of America

40 39 38 37 36 35 34 33 32

NANCY DREW and colophon are registered trademarks of
Simon & Schuster, Inc.

NANCY DREW: GIRL DETECTIVE is a trademark of
Simon & Schuster, Inc.

Library of Congress Control Number 2003109056

ISBN-13: 978-0-689-86568-8
ISBN-10: 0-689-86568-6

0710 OFF

Contents

Questions Without Answers

Okay, **Miss Drew. What** is it this time? Did you stumble upon a crime ring? Witness a dognapping? Solve a few murders I didn't know about?"

I looked over at the man who was speaking to me and immediately recognized Chief McGinnis, the head of the River Heights Police Department. He was standing on the sidewalk with his arms folded across his chest, one bushy, grayish brown eyebrow raised.

I'd wandered right past the police station without realizing it. I couldn't really blame the chief for seeming wary of my approach. I have sort of a reputation around town for solving puzzles, crimes, and mysteries in general—often before the police can figure them out. And that doesn't always make me the chief's favorite person.

"Don't worry, Chief McGinnis," I said with a smile. "The only mystery on my plate right now is figuring out what to get my dad for his birthday."

"Oh!" The chief's expression suddenly changed from slightly sour suspicion to genuine interest. "Carson has a birthday coming up, does he?"

I sometimes think the only reason Chief McGinnis puts up with my amateur detecting at all is because he respects my father so much. Everyone in town does. Dad is the most successful attorney in River Heights, and possibly in the entire midwestern U.S., but that's only part of the reason. The other part is that he's just as honest and smart and caring as he is successful.

"That's right," I told the chief, pushing a few strands of my strawberry blond hair out of my eyes. "It's this Thursday. We're having a little get-together for him that evening, if you'd like to come."

The chief looked pleased to be invited. "Well, I'll have to check my schedule," he said. "I'll let you know." He glanced at his watch. "I'd better get back inside now. Take care, Nancy."

I gave him a wave and walked on. I'd spent the last couple of hours wandering all over the River Heights shopping district. I couldn't believe Dad's birthday was only three days away and I still had no idea what to get him. It's definitely a challenge to shop for Dad.

I knew he would be happy with whatever I got him, but I wanted to make sure his gift was something really special. He's been both father and mother to me ever since my mother died when I was three, and I like to let him know how much I appreciate him.

A couple of doors down from the police station, I glanced into the large plate-glass window of a small shop called the Psychic's Parlor. Inside I spotted a petite, dark-haired woman sitting at a table with a cup of tea. It was Lucia Gonsalvo, the shop's owner and sole employee. She smiled and gestured for me to come inside.

The copper wind chimes over the door tinkled softly as I entered the shop, which was painted in warm shades of red and gold and smelled pleasantly of incense and mint. Lucia hurried over to give me a hug, almost knocking off the red velvet turban she was wearing. Her dozens of bracelets and necklaces jingled with her every move, blending with the sound of the wind chimes.

"Nancy!" she exclaimed in heavily accented, but flawless, English. Nobody knew exactly where Lucia had come from, but she had been in River Heights for at least ten years. "What a pleasant surprise."

"What, you mean you didn't foresee that I would be coming?" I teased.

Lucia smiled and waggled a finger at me. "Now,

now," she said. "You shouldn't make fun of the fates. It's bad luck."

I grinned. Lucia and I have been good friends ever since Dad represented her in a dispute with her landlord. Thanks to his intervention, the two sides had come to an amicable agreement, and Lucia's psychic shop had been able to remain in its longtime location on River Street between the police station and a big antique shop.

I sat down in a plush armchair at the wooden table in the center of the small room. "Okay, then predict this for me: What am I going to get Dad for his birthday? Because right now, I have no idea."

Lucia shook her head. "Now, Nancy, I was only joking. You know this is all just for fun—I can't *really* tell you what will happen." She bustled over to the teapot on a fabric-draped side table and poured me a cup of tea.

"Thanks," I said as she set it in front of me. "And yes, I know—you're always telling me that. But it would be a lot more convenient if you could just peek into your crystal ball once in a while and tell me what's going to happen. Like when I have a tough mystery to solve, for instance."

"I can certainly predict what would happen if I *could* tell you," Lucia said, sitting down across from me. "You wouldn't like it—it would make it far too easy to solve the mysteries, and that wouldn't be any fun at all."

I had to admit she had a point. Ever since I was a young girl, mysteries have seemed to find me. And I like it that way. There's nothing I love more than puzzling through clues, figuring out connections and motives to solve a tough case. Chief McGinnis isn't the only one who gets noticed either. I'm pretty well known around River Heights for my amateur sleuthing abilities. Sometimes people even seek me out to ask for help with sticky or mysterious problems.

"Okay, fine," I told Lucia. "But even if you can't magically predict what I should get for Dad, maybe you can help me think of ideas."

"Ah, that's very different," Lucia said. "I'd love to help if I can. Have you considered stereo equipment? Or maybe some new CDs—I seem to remember that he loves classical music, right?"

"That's the problem." I sighed. "If he wants anything like that, he just goes out and buys it himself."

"All right, then," Lucia said. "We'll have to be more creative. What about a subscription to a new magazine, or . . ." She paused for a moment and looked out the window. "Something's wrong."

"Tell me about it," I said, stirring my tea. "If I don't come up with some good ideas soon, I'll be giving Dad tube socks for his birthday. Or maybe a tie—that's what I usually got him when I was a kid." I shrugged. "Not very original, but he always claimed to like them."

"No. Something is *very* wrong."

I blinked, realizing that Lucia wasn't playing around anymore—her voice had suddenly turned deadly serious.

"Huh?" I twisted around to see what was going on outside. "What is it?"

It was a little after lunchtime on a sleepy late-summer Monday, which meant that the street was nearly deserted. The only sign of life I could see was an ordinary-looking African-American couple standing on the sidewalk across from Lucia's shop.

Or maybe they weren't so ordinary after all. As I watched, the woman—an attractive female in her forties, dressed in a trim navy pantsuit—tugged on the man's sleeve, looking distraught. The man, who appeared to be her husband, was tall and lean, with gray at his temples and an expression of determination on his handsome face as he stared across the street. The woman grabbed his arm again, but he shook his head and pulled away.

I tilted my head to one side, trying to figure out why the woman looked so familiar. I was pretty sure I'd seen her somewhere before, but I couldn't put my finger on when or where. Was she one of Dad's clients? A local merchant or businesswoman? Some-one from one of my volunteer groups?

Before I could figure out the answer, the man took a step into the street. The woman cried out. I couldn't hear what she was saying from inside Lucia's shop, but I could see her mouth move. She gestured wildly, still seeming very distraught.

I glanced over at Lucia, wondering if the people were regular clients of hers. The man certainly seemed determined to come over toward the shop.

"There is something very serious happening with those people," Lucia said grimly. "*Very* serious."

"Do you know them?" I asked.

She shook her head. "I don't have to know them to see that they are in trouble."

I shrugged, wondering if Lucia was teasing me again, pretending to see into the future or something. But when I glanced at her, her expression was grim. She seemed convinced that something unusual was going on with the couple outside. In my years of sleuthing I've learned it's wise never to jump to con-clusions without enough evidence. And, at that mo-ment, I just didn't see evidence of anything much more than a minor disagreement.

"Well, I suppose they *could* be in serious trouble," I said, trying to be tactful. "But it's also possible that they're just a married couple having an argument."

"No," Lucia said firmly. "It is more. Much more."

I glanced at the couple again, a little surprised by her certainty. Despite the somewhat wacky way that she makes her living, Lucia is usually pretty sensible and perceptive. What made her think that we were witnessing anything more than a perfectly ordinary argument? Was she just being dramatic, or was I missing something?

That's when I realized that the man wasn't looking toward the psychic shop after all. As he took another step into the street, he stared directly at a building just to our left—the police station.

I raised my eyebrows curiously. That changed things a little, didn't it?

But I wasn't going to find out how just then. The woman finally appeared to prevail. She pulled at the man's arm again, and this time I saw his shoulders slump with what looked like defeat. His face crumpled, and he swiped at his eyes with the back of one hand. Turning around, he walked rapidly toward a late-model blue sedan parked at the curb. He and the woman both climbed inside.

"Weird," I muttered under my breath as a puff of exhaust blew out from the rear of the car.

The sedan pulled away from the curb with a screech of tires—and a second later, it was gone.

2

A Surprising Reaction

How about a bathrobe?"

What?" I blinked at Lucia, momentarily confused. Then I realized she had returned to our previous topic of conversation. "Oh," I said, glancing out the window again. "Um, I think he already has one that he likes."

I stared out at the empty street. I don't really believe in psychics and that sort of thing, but I do believe that I have sort of a sixth sense about when people are in trouble. Dad says it's really just keen attention to detail combined with a quick mind. My best friends, Bess and George, usually just call it a crazy hunch. I don't know how to explain it myself, but when I feel it, I'm hardly ever wrong. And I was

9

feeling it now—it had hit me as soon as I'd seen that man staring toward the police station with that sad, worried expression on his face.

Just then the chimes above the door tinkled. A short, rather plump man with neat but sparse brown hair had entered the shop. I immediately recognized Harold Safer, the owner of the local cheese shop who lives a few blocks from me.

"Good afternoon, Mr. Safer," Lucia greeted him warmly. "Have you come for a reading?"

Mr. Safer smiled. "I have indeed," he said. "I have an important question about my shop, and it's worth stepping out for a moment for some otherworldly advice. I'm trying to decide whether to branch out into buffalo-milk cheese. The last time I was in New York, I noticed it was all the rage in the more exclusive cheese shops there. Oh, hello, Nancy."

"Hi, Mr. Safer." I smiled at him. He's always been one of my favorite neighbors. Aside from cheese, his life revolves around his two great passions: sunsets and Broadway musicals.

"Nancy, you'd like to try buffalo-milk cheese, wouldn't you?" Mr. Safer asked me. "It wouldn't be too weird for you, would it?"

Lucia winked at me. "That could be the answer to your problem, Nancy," she said. "You could get your father some nice, exotic buffalo-milk cheese for his birthday. That's something he doesn't have already, right?"

I laughed and stood up, carrying my teacup over to the side table. "Excuse me," I said. "I'd better get going and leave you two to your reading. Lucia, you just reminded me that I still have some important shopping to do."

"All right," Lucia said. "Thanks for stopping in and keeping me company, Nancy." She sounded cheerful and seemed to have forgotten all about the incident we'd witnessed out in the street. But I hadn't forgotten.

After quickly inviting both of them to my father's birthday party, I headed for the door. "Thanks for the tea, Lucia," I added. "I hope I'll see you on Thursday night. You too, Mr. Safer. And good luck with the buffalo cheese thing."

After leaving Lucia's shop, I wandered down the block, glancing into store windows as I passed. But my mind wasn't really on shopping anymore. I was distracted by what I had seen before, though I wasn't quite sure why. It was like the little scene kept nagging at my mind, almost calling out to me. . . .

I blinked, suddenly realizing that someone really *was* calling out my name. Turning around, I saw Bess and George jogging toward me.

"It's about time you heard us," George panted as she skidded to a stop in front of me. As usual, she was dressed in casual, sporty clothes that matched her boyish nickname. She ran a hand over her close-cropped dark hair and scowled at me. "We've been shouting at you for the past three blocks."

Her cousin Bess, a pretty blonde with sparkling blue eyes and a peaches-and-cream complexion, rolled her eyes. "Don't exaggerate, George," she chided. She glanced at me. "Seriously though, Nancy, what's with you? We thought you'd gone deaf or something. Didn't you hear us?"

"No," I admitted sheepishly. "Guess I was thinking about something."

The cousins exchanged a glance.

"Uh-oh," Bess said playfully. "Does this mean what I think it means?"

"Okay, spill it." George folded her arms over her chest. "Did you find yourself another mystery, Nancy?"

I giggled. My friends knew me way too well.

"I'm not sure it's really a mystery," I told them. "Not at the moment anyway. Right now it's just something weird I saw a few minutes ago. . . ."

I started to fill them in on what had happened outside Lucia's shop. As I was describing the woman, I suddenly gasped and interrupted myself.

"I've got it!" I cried. "I just remembered who she is—Heather Simmons!"

Bess blinked. "You mean the woman who's been talking about running for mayor?"

I nodded, pleased that I'd finally identified the woman. I didn't know her personally, but I'd seen her picture in the *River Heights Bugle*—the local newspaper that happened to be published by my boyfriend's father. Ned often worked for his dad at the *Bugle* during summer vacations, and that year he'd written several stories about the upcoming mayor's race. Although actually, as he liked to put it, it hadn't looked like much of a race until recently. He'd also mentioned to me that Heather Simmons's husband, Clay, had taught a class he'd taken at the local university the semester before.

"I still can't believe Mayor Strong is really retiring," George mused as the three of us continued strolling down the block. "He's been around practically since we were all in diapers."

"I know," I said. "And I think a lot of people will be voting for Heather Simmons to replace him if she really does enter the race. She's very qualified for the job."

"Besides, a lot of people aren't too thrilled with the only other choice so far," George added. "I mean, for one thing, Morris Granger has only lived here for about five minutes. I heard he still has homes in about five other cities! When *did* he buy that town house of his anyway?"

Bess wrinkled her nose. "I don't know. But count me in as one of the less-than thrilled," she said. "The last thing this city needs is some superrich corporate type like him swooping in and taking over."

"He probably only wants the job to make it easier to take over Rackham Industries," George agreed, referring to the local computer company and the biggest employer in River Heights. "Then he'll move the whole company to some kind of offshore tax haven and leave this place destitute."

I laughed. "Hold on," I said. "You're making him sound like some kind of dastardly deviant. Don't forget, he's already done some good things for the town."

George shrugged. "Yeah, yeah," she said, kicking at a pebble on the sidewalk. "So he built a new public skating rink and a couple of playgrounds. Big deal. That's chump change for a guy like him."

But Bess looked conflicted. "He's starting work on the new Granger Children's Hospital, too," she reminded George. "Remember? It's that new construction site over on Union Street."

Suddenly I stopped short, noticing a display in the art-store window we were passing. "Hey," I said, pointing. "Do you think Dad might like something like that? He likes modern art, right?"

"You mean that painting of a big gray blob with purple polka dots?" George looked skeptical. "Let me guess, Nancy. This means you still don't have any good ideas for a birthday present."

I grinned. "You got that right," I admitted. "I've been walking all over town today in search of the perfect gift, but nothing seems quite right. He's always hard to shop for, but for some reason this year it's harder than ever."

Bess looked sympathetic. "Did you ask Hannah for help?"

"Yep. No dice." Hannah Gruen, our longtime housekeeper, knows Dad about as well as anyone. But she hadn't had any brilliant ideas either. She was taking the easy way out herself—her gift to Dad was going to be fixing all his favorite foods for his party on Thursday night.

"All right, what about asking Ned?" Bess suggested. "He's a guy—he should be able to help you figure something out."

"I asked him," I said. "The only thing he could come up with were golf clubs or CDs. But Dad just bought himself a new set of clubs a couple of months ago. And he has so many CDs, I wouldn't even know where to start."

George's eyes lit up. "I know!" she said. "Why not

get him a gift certificate to the music store? Then he can pick out his own CDs."

"I guess," I said without much enthusiasm. "If I can't come up with anything else, I'll probably do that. It just seems kind of impersonal, you know?"

Bess looked over at me as we walked on. "Sounds like you're getting pretty discouraged."

"Nancy Drew 'discouraged'?" George exclaimed. "Never! I won't believe it. Not the famous amateur sleuth who's tracked down more criminals than the entire River Heights Police Department. Not the determined investigator who won't rest until every single clue is uncovered. Not the girl who wouldn't give up until she cracked the code of Bess's diary."

I couldn't help laughing. "Very funny," I said, giving George a shove. "But you're right. I'm not giving up. I'm going to find the perfect birthday gift for Dad if it kills me!"

Unfortunately I still hadn't solved the mystery of Dad's birthday gift by the time I headed home for dinner. My head was spinning with all the possibilities I'd considered and rejected: designer clothing, tropical fish, sports memorabilia, electronic equipment. . . . While Dad's many interests and hobbies provided numerous possibilities, nothing seemed original or special enough to make the perfect birthday gift from his only daughter.

I let myself into my house. The dim coolness of the front hall was a welcome relief after being in the heat. "Hello, I'm home!" I called.

"Hi, Nancy," Hannah's familiar voice returned from the direction of the dining room. "Hurry up. Dinner's just about on the table."

As I went into the powder room off the front hall to wash my hands, I caught a whiff of the tantalizing odor of Hannah's famous squash and mushroom soup. That made me feel a little better. But I couldn't help but continue to think about my fruitless shopping expedition as I hurried into the dining room a few minutes later and took my usual seat at the polished mahogany table.

Dad and Hannah were already seated. "Hi, Nancy," Dad greeted me, glancing up from his soup. "How was your day?"

"Okay, I guess." The words came out sounding a little gloomy, even to myself. I forced a smile, not wanting Dad to guess why I was feeling so down in the dumps. "Oh, actually something sort of interesting—and a little weird—happened this afternoon."

"What's that, dear?" Hannah asked, passing me the soup tureen.

I helped myself to a bowl of the thick, ginger-scented soup. "I was downtown—er, just doing a little window shopping," I said. "I stopped in to visit with

Lucia Gonsalvo in her shop. While we were having tea, we spotted a couple on the street outside. I thought they looked familiar, but at first I couldn't remember who they were."

"Oh, really?" Dad turned and winked playfully at Hannah. "Uh-oh. Sounds very mysterious so far. The summer heat must be affecting Nancy's brain."

I grinned. "Maybe a little," I joked. I paused for a moment to blow on my soup, because it was still too hot to eat. "Since it took me about *ten minutes* to realize that it was Heather and Clay Simmons. You know, the woman who's been talking about running for mayor of River Heights, and her husband, who teaches over at the university? But the weird part was, Lucia was *sure* there was something terribly wrong by the way they were acting—and I'm not sure she wasn't . . ."

My words trailed off as Dad's soup spoon clattered loudly against the edge of his bowl, bounced off the table, and fell to the floor. "Excuse me," he muttered, diving down to retrieve it.

I stared at him in surprise when he sat up again. His face—which a moment ago had looked relaxed and jovial—was suddenly hardened into an expression of shock.

3

Mystery or Not?

I was startled at the sudden change in Dad's demeanor. But I quickly realized that there was only one likely explanation: The Simmonses must be clients. Dad was always careful to respect the attorney/client relationship, and I knew better than to press him when he got like that.

Anyway, maybe that explained away the whole "mystery," I thought as Hannah bustled off to the kitchen to fetch Dad a clean spoon. Maybe Mr. and Mrs. Simmons were having some sort of legal trouble, and that's why they had been arguing on the street. If so, this was starting to look like a serious case of None of My Business.

Clearing my throat, I decided it was time to change the subject. Since the Simmonses were still in

19

my mind, I started to think about their daughter. Leslie Simmons was just a couple of years younger than I was. I didn't know her that well, but everyone in town knew that she was a talented pianist and one of the most promising musicians River Heights had seen in a long time.

"Hey, speaking of the Simmons family," I said as Hannah returned and placed a spoon on the table next to Dad. "I heard the other day that Leslie is trying out for that scholarship the conservatory is awarding to the most promising high school musician."

Dad had just raised a spoonful of soup to his mouth. At my comment, he almost choked on it. The spoon clattered into his bowl again as he pounded on his own chest, coughing and sputtering.

I stared at him. What was going on? Obviously the entire Simmons family was a sensitive subject for him at the moment. But why? He regularly represented a lot of people in town, from Lucia Gonsalvo to Harold Safer to the outgoing mayor, and he didn't start choking every time one of their names came up. Whatever was going on with the Simmons family, it had to be big.

When Dad got his breath back, he dabbed at his mouth with his napkin. Then he met my gaze briefly before looking away.

"Sorry, Hannah," he said in a slightly raspy voice.

"I just got distracted there for a moment. Nothing to do with your soup—it's delicious, as always."

I could take a hint. It was clearly time to drop the whole topic of the Simmons family.

"Yes, it's great," I added, smiling at Hannah and taking a quick sip of my own soup. "What kind of mushrooms do you put in it again?"

After that the conversation at the dinner table proceeded more normally. But I was still thinking about the earlier incident as I helped Hannah clear the table. That little sixth sense of mine was tingling—not to mention my curiosity. Maybe it was none of my business, but I couldn't help wondering if the Simmonses were in trouble, and if what I'd witnessed that afternoon had something to do with it.

As soon as I could, I excused myself and hurried upstairs. I closed my bedroom door, picked up the phone on my bedside table, and dialed George's number.

"Okay, so what's the big emergency?" George teased as she swung open her front door a few minutes later.

Bess appeared in the doorway behind her. She looked curious. "Yeah, Nancy," she added. "I was planning to give myself a pedicure tonight."

"Sorry to tear you away from such exciting plans," I said, only half kidding. Bess takes grooming and beauty treatments very seriously. "Let's go upstairs, and I'll tell you everything."

George led the way down the hall to the stairs. The Faynes' house is a comfortable, rambling colonial where George lives with her parents, her older brother, Sebastian, when he's home from college, and her younger brother, Scott. Soon the three of us were entering her messy, chaotic bedroom. It was a large room, but it seemed much smaller because of the masses of power cords crisscrossing the floor, and the computer equipment and other electrical gadgets stacked on every possible surface.

Bess blinked and looked around at the mess. "Hey," she said in surprise. "You cleaned up in here!"

"Yeah, a little." George flopped onto her unmade bed. "Okay, enough chitchat. What's going on, Nancy?"

I perched on the edge of George's desk chair, which I had to share with a set of stereo speakers and a spare modem. "It's about Heather Simmons," I began.

"That again?" George interrupted, rolling her eyes. "Come on, Nancy. A woman arguing with her husband does not a mystery make—not even when that woman happens to be running for mayor."

"I know, I know." I held up my hand to stop her. "But listen to this. . . ."

I quickly described my innocent comments at dinner, and Dad's extreme reactions. As I did, my mind kept turning over what I was saying, poking and prodding at it to try to make sense of it. That's one of the reasons I like it when my friends help me with cases. Talking to them about weird things and puzzling clues often helps me figure things out faster.

Bess looked uncertain. "Okay," she said when I was finished. "So that tells us . . . what? That they're probably his clients. So? That doesn't necessarily mean there's a mystery brewing."

Meanwhile George was licking her lips. "Do you think Hannah has any of that soup left over?" she asked. "I remember it well—she brought it to that potluck thing at the fire station. It was delicious!"

I sighed. For such a thin girl, George had a practically bottomless stomach. It killed Bess to watch her cousin eat like a pig and never gain an ounce, while Bess herself remained pleasantly plump.

"It may be nothing," I told Bess. "But why would Dad freak out so much over an ordinary client? Why did he look more upset than ever when I mentioned Leslie?"

"I can answer that one," George said, apparently forgetting about her stomach for a moment. "Maybe whatever legal thing they're dealing with has to do with her."

"Like what?" Bess asked.

George shrugged. "Well, everyone says she's a shoo-in for that music prize thing, right?"

"You mean the scholarship to the conservatory?" I said. "I suppose that's true. She's a great pianist. I can't imagine anyone else in town who could beat her out for the scholarship."

"So maybe that's it," George said. "Maybe her folks want to make sure they're not going to be signing anything they don't want to sign—you know, if she wins."

I thought about that for a second. "Maybe," I said. "But why would Dad seem upset about that? Besides, I have a hunch there may be something much stranger going on here."

Bess giggled. "Aha, I see what's going on here. We're dealing with a patented Nancy Drew hunch. We might as well just give up right now."

I smiled patiently as George burst out laughing. My friends love to tease me about my hunches.

"Very funny," I said. "Anyway, I really do have a hunch about this, and I was hoping you guys could help." I smiled pleadingly at George. "Feel like doing a little snooping on the computer?"

I knew I wouldn't have to ask twice, no matter how skeptical George might be. She loves anything having to do with the computer. She's practically a computer genius—she can find anything on the

24

Internet, and has been the information systems manager for her mother's catering business since we were all in junior high.

Soon she was online, scrolling through her search results for any information on Heather and Clay Simmons. I stood up and peeked over her shoulder at the screen.

"Sorry the monitor's so small," George said, glancing up at me. "If I had the money, I'd definitely get a nice, big flat-screen. . . ."

Bess and I exchanged an amused look. George is almost always short of money. As soon as she gets a few dollars together, she can't resist spending it on a new video game or DVD, or the latest gadget she sees down at Riverside Electronics.

Even on the small screen, it soon became obvious that the search wasn't going to turn up anything juicy. Most of the entries led to newspaper articles from the *Bugle* about Heather's comments to the school board or Clay's speeches in front of local groups.

I pointed to a link on the *Bugle*'s homepage for the River Heights official town Web site. "Let's check that out," I suggested. "Maybe it will tell us something interesting."

George clicked on the link. Soon the screen was flashing a photo of the town hall, along with a list of topics, from local school information to sources for town maps. "Anything strike your fancy?" George asked, the cursor hovering next to the list.

"Let's check out 'Latest News,'" I suggested.

The page that came up featured recent press releases and other articles, as well as an archive of past stories. I leaned closer as George scrolled slowly down the list, squinting to read the tiny print.

"Look," I said, pointing to an item near the top of the page. "This mentions the mayor's retirement, and the election for his successor."

Bess was reading too. "Looks like Morris Granger has already filed the paperwork to run for mayor," she said, pointing to a section of text about halfway down the screen. "It says he's the only one so far. Oh! But look—here it says that 'another citizen' has declared an intent to run but hasn't turned in the rest of the necessary paperwork yet."

"That must be Heather Simmons," I mused. "And look—it says the deadline for the paperwork is this coming Friday. That's interesting."

"Interesting? Maybe," George agreed. "But a mystery? Not really."

I shrugged. "You may be right. She's probably still working on it," I said. "It's only Monday. She has all week to get it in." But my mind was buzzing along, trying to fit that bit of information in with what I already knew.

George was clicking on another link. A second later a colorful site loaded on the screen. The headline read, "River Heights Music Conservatory." Just under that, it said, "Coming Soon: Check this page for results of the High School Talent Search scholarship competition."

The name of the competition was in a different color from the other words. "Is that a link?" I asked George, pointing to it.

She clicked on it. Another page came up. This one included a list of alphabetized names and audition times.

"Scroll down and see if Leslie Simmons is on the list," I told George.

Bess gave me a perplexed look. "Of course she is," she said. "Everyone knows she's trying out for the scholarship."

"Here it is," George said, peering at the screen. "'Simmons, L.: eight fifteen A.M.' It's right here below—oops!" She giggled.

"What's so funny?" I asked, leaning over her shoulder for a better look.

George pointed to a name on the list. "Check it out. The name above Leslie Simmons is 'Sharon, D.' But when I first looked at it, I thought it said, 'Shannon, D.'"

Bess and I both laughed, realizing immediately

why George had found that funny. The three of us had gone through school with a girl named Deirdre Shannon, and she was just about the *last* person we would expect to see trying out for a music scholarship. Deirdre was pretty and rich, and she figured that was enough. She rarely put much effort into anything other than her hair, makeup, and wardrobe. Oh, and guys, of course—she was *always* turning up with a new date on her arm, not to mention flirting her head off with Ned every chance she got.

"Didn't Deirdre play the flute in elementary school?" Bess said.

"Yes," I recalled. "For about ten seconds!"

As my friends continued to joke around at Deirdre's expense, I returned my attention to the computer screen. *Simmons, L.* I stared at the name thoughtfully, remembering how strongly Dad had reacted to my mention of Leslie's name.

"Hey, George," I said, interrupting whatever she was saying to Bess. "Can you check out one more site?"

"Sure. What?"

"River Heights High School," I said. "I want to see if we can find out anything more about Leslie Simmons."

Bess cocked her head at me as George went to work. "Why?" she asked. "Even if she has something to do with this so-called mystery, what's the high school home page going to tell you? It's summer, remember? School's out."

George glanced up at her as the home page loaded. "Yeah, but the school bulletin board is still active all summer," she reminded Bess. "A lot of kids keep in touch that way, remember?"

Bess wrinkled her nose. She muttered something under her breath that sounded suspiciously like, "Yeah, the geeks, maybe."

I swallowed a laugh as George shot her cousin a dirty look. Then I leaned over and pointed to a link. "Look, there's the bulletin board," I said. "Let's see if Leslie has checked in lately."

It turned out that she had—quite a lot, actually. There were all kinds of entries from her. Some were just chitchat, while others had to do with her music studies.

"Look, she's been going to music camp over at the university's performing arts building," Bess said, pointing to one entry.

George nodded. "I knew that already," she said. "My mom wants to go to their recital—I think it's this week. She loves to hear Leslie Simmons play."

"Interesting," I said. "And look, here's something even more interesting. Leslie's most recent bulletin board entry was at two thirty-eight P.M. on Saturday—two days ago. There's nothing since then, even though she was posting several times per day up until then."

George shrugged. "So?" she said. "She's got a big week coming up—first the recital, then the audition on Thursday. She's probably practicing twenty-four seven."

"Maybe." I stared at the screen. "It's just a little weird, that's all."

Bess narrowed her blue eyes at me. "Nancy, I know that look," she said. "You're coming up with a theory, aren't you? Come on, spill it."

I smiled. Bess was right—I was starting to think I might know why the Simmonses had looked so upset earlier. But I wasn't quite ready to share yet.

"In a minute," I told my friends. "First, let's take a little ride over to the Simmons house, okay?"

Bess and George exchanged a perplexed glance. Then they both sighed.

"All right, come on," Bess said. "I'll drive."

Soon we were cruising down a pleasant, tree-lined residential block in the eastern section of River Heights. The streetlights had just come on, even though dusk had barely thickened the shadows beneath the shrubs and playsets in the neatly tended yards. I pointed to a green-shuttered white clapboard house about halfway down the block.

"That's their house," I said. "I sold raffle tickets door-to-door a couple of years ago for the hospital fundraiser, and I remember talking to Mr. Simmons in front of his house. He bought five tickets."

George leaned forward from the backseat of the car to give me a funny look. "You know, sometimes it's downright scary the way your mind files things away, Nancy."

Bess idled at the curb in front of the house. "Well?" she said. "What do you want to do now? Should I park?"

I bit my lip, not quite sure how to proceed now that we were there. I stared at the house. There were two cars in the driveway, and several lights were on inside. Through the large picture window to the left of the front door, I could see a grand piano.

"No, just wait here a sec," I said, reaching for the door handle. "I want to check on something."

I hopped out of the car before my friends could ask any more questions. The theory that had been forming in my mind still hadn't totally jelled yet, but my sixth sense was tingling like crazy.

Not knowing exactly what I was going to say, I moved up the front walk and rapped on the door. A moment later I heard footsteps inside, and Heather Simmons answered.

She gasped at me and looked very startled. Even

though we'd never actually met, she obviously recognized me. "Nancy Drew!" she blurted out. "Did your father—" She gulped, clearly struggling to regain her composure. "I mean, hello. Please come in. What can I do for you this evening?"

I pasted a friendly smile on my face as I stepped into the foyer. "Sorry to bother you this late, Mrs. Simmons," I said. "I'm just out reminding people that the River Heights Animal Shelter will be doing a pet adopt-a-thon next weekend at Bluff View Park. There will be games and door prizes and all sorts of fun stuff. I hope you and your family will come out and support us."

That was all true enough. I volunteered once a month at the shelter, and we were all excited about the event. But even while I was talking, I was shooting curious glances around at the inside of the house. I wasn't sure exactly what I was looking for—any clue, any small hint that might confirm my growing suspicions. My gaze darted over the half-open coat closet in the foyer, the large arched entryway into the living room, the dark-colored grand piano in front of the window, the last rays of sunlight gleaming on the slightly grayish keyboard. . . .

"Oh!" Heather Simmons blinked, seeming distracted. "Well, thank you, Nancy. I'm sure we'll try to make it if we can."

"That's . . . great." I was suddenly distracted myself. I had just spotted it—the clue I needed. "Um, okay, then. I'd better be going," I added. "Thanks for your support."

Mrs. Simmons looked a little confused at my abrupt farewell, but she didn't seem eager to change my mind about leaving. As soon as the door clicked shut behind me, I sprinted for Bess's car. I flung the door open and jumped inside.

"I was right," I said breathlessly. "I just saw something in there that confirms what I was thinking: Leslie Simmons has been kidnapped!"

4

Kidnapped!

H uh?" **Bess and George** said at the same time, their faces registering identical expressions of surprise.

"It all makes perfect sense," I said, my words practically tumbling over each other in my eagerness to explain my theory. "The deadline for filing those papers to run for mayor is this Friday, right?"

"Uh-huh," George said. "So?"

"So don't you get it?" I exclaimed. "Someone obviously wants to distract Heather Simmons so she won't be able to file!"

"Obviously," George said, in a tone that indicated that she thought I was off my rocker.

Bess looked troubled. "But who would do something like that?"

"Why, Morris Granger, of course!" I said. "He's the

only possible suspect. He's got the money and the power and connections to pull off something like this. And I'm sure he'd love nothing more than to run for mayor unopposed."

"Whoa . . . hold the phone, here." George held up both hands. "Back up a second, Nancy. What happened in there to lead you to this, er, *interesting* conclusion?" She gestured toward the Simmons house.

"Oh, right. I forgot to tell you that." I poked Bess in the arm. "Let's get going. We probably look kind of suspicious sitting out here in front of their house."

As Bess drove back toward George's house, I filled my friends in on my brief conversation with Mrs. Simmons. I mentioned how distracted she had seemed while talking with me.

"Don't tell me that's your big clue?" George said skeptically. "There better be more than that—or you might have to give back your World's Greatest Amateur Sleuth title."

I grinned and shook my head. "There's definitely more," I assured her. "I was trying to look around while I chatted with Mrs. Simmons—you know, to see if I could spot anything suspicious or out of place."

"Like a big ransom note cut out of newspaper letters?" Bess giggled. "Let me guess: It was tacked up on the wall and signed in blood."

"Very funny," I said. "No, it was nothing as obvious as that. It was the piano. I was sort of staring at it out of the corner of my eye, thinking that it was weird that Leslie wouldn't be sitting there practicing with the recital and auditions coming up."

Bess shrugged and glanced over at me before returning her gaze to the road. "Even piano prodigies have to take a break sometime," she said. "Maybe she was in the kitchen having dinner. Or taking a shower. Or out with friends."

"Maybe, but that's not the point," I said. "The point is, I noticed that the piano keys looked funny—they're supposed to be ivory, right? But these looked sort of grayish. That's when I realized they were dusty."

"Dusty?" George repeated from the backseat, still sounding perplexed.

I nodded. "Dusty. And that means they haven't been touched in at least a couple of days."

"That *is* kind of weird." Bess clicked on her turn signal as she reached an intersection. "But wait, I still don't get what all this has to do with Morris Granger and the rest of the stuff you said."

I explained the scenario again patiently. "There's no way Leslie would go without practicing that long with a recital coming up, let alone that important audition. She must not have been home for the past couple of days at least—which matches up with what we saw on the school's Internet bulletin board. She's been missing from there for two days too."

"Right," George said. "But that doesn't mean she's been kidnapped. Maybe she's off visiting her grandparents or something."

"It's possible," I admitted. "But I don't think so. It just ties in too perfectly with my dad's weird reaction to Leslie's name, and also what I saw on the street earlier today. I think Mr. and Mrs. Simmons were arguing about whether or not they should go to the police. Her parents are afraid to report Leslie's disappearance. Maybe they received a ransom note or a phone call warning them not to tell anyone." I shrugged. "They obviously decided not to involve the police. But they must have decided to risk talking to Dad—probably to get his advice about what to do. That would explain his reaction."

"I guess that could make sense," Bess said as she pulled to the curb in front of George's house. "Your dad probably wouldn't freak out like that if they were just regular clients coming to him about some ordinary thing. But I still don't see how Granger fits in."

"I'm getting to that," I said. "See, we know from checking the town Web site that he's the only one who's officially running for mayor as of now. And if local gossip holds true, the only other person thinking of throwing her hat in the ring is Heather Simmons.

But she needs to get that paperwork in before Friday's deadline. What better way to distract her from doing that than by kidnapping her daughter?"

"But that seems so crazy," George protested, leaning on the front seat to talk to us. "It's taking a huge risk. If Granger did something like that and got caught, his political career would sink faster than an anvil in the river."

I nodded. That was the only part of my theory that was still bothering me. "I know," I said. "But a guy like Granger is probably used to taking big risks—gambling on big stock purchases and corporate takeovers. Maybe he figures the payoff is worth it. Mayors are powerful. If he gets elected, he'll be in a great position to affect all sorts of stuff at Rackham Industries and arrange a takeover on his terms."

I could tell that Bess and George still weren't totally convinced, but they both agreed to help me investigate. If Leslie really was in trouble, we all wanted to help.

"First things first," George said as we all climbed out of the car. She pulled out her cell phone. "Let's find out for sure if Leslie really has been MIA for the past couple of days."

"Good idea," Bess said. "Who are you going to call though? Her parents aren't going to tell you, even if it's true."

"Duh," George said. "But she's supposed to be going to music camp, remember? We can call them and ask if she showed up today. I'll get the number from Directory Assistance."

By the time we reached George's front steps, we had our answer. Leslie Simmons had been absent from music camp that day—the first time she'd missed a day since camp started.

Bess paused outside the door, looking somber. "Okay, you guys," she said. "This is starting to get serious. If Nancy's theory is right, this means big trouble. We should call the police right now and tell them what we know."

"Bess has a point," George agreed. "Kidnapping is serious stuff, Nance. The cops should be the ones to handle it."

I chewed my lower lip. "I'm not so sure," I said slowly. "I see what you guys are saying, and I agree that this is serious. But that's exactly why I think we need to be careful. I mean, think about it—do you really expect Chief McGinnis to believe all this if the Simmonses haven't called him themselves?" I thought back to my encounter with him earlier that day and grimaced, imagining how the conversation my friends were suggesting might go.

What a surprise, Miss Drew, the chief might say dryly. *So you've turned up a kidnapping all of a sudden.*

Must be having a boring summer, eh? Why don't you take up a normal hobby. Imaginary crimes aren't a worthy pastime for Carson Drew's only daughter. . . .

"Okay, maybe not," Bess said. From the expression on her face, I guessed she was probably imagining a similar conversation. "But we should at least try to do the right thing."

"But *is* it the right thing?" I said. "If Leslie's parents haven't reported her missing, there must be a reason—some kind of ransom note, or instructions to keep quiet, backed up with threats of some kind. We don't want to put Leslie in more danger."

George looked uncertain. "You don't really think Granger would . . ." Her voice trailed off.

"We don't know what he might do," I said. "In fact, I think it's time to do a little more snooping into our possible future mayor. Come on, let's hit the computer again."

Soon we were back at George's computer, digging through the many online mentions of Morris Granger. We turned up plenty of information about his companies, his real estate holdings, and much more. George had been right about his homes in other parts of the country; he owned property in several midwestern states, apartments in Chicago and New York City, a beach estate in Florida, and a town house in River Heights.

"Yikes," Bess said. "What if he's shipped Leslie off to one of those places? We'd never be able to find her without help from the police."

"I doubt he'd do that," I said. "I mean, I'm sure he doesn't really want to hurt her, or keep her forever. He's probably planning to release her as soon as the paperwork deadline passes and his unopposed run is a sure thing. So it makes sense that he'd keep her someplace local."

"But if he releases Leslie, won't she be able to turn him in as the kidnapper?" George pointed out.

I shrugged. "Only if she knows he was behind it," I replied. "And I seriously doubt that a rich, powerful man like Morris Granger would get anywhere near the dirty work himself. He probably hired some icky underworld-criminal types to grab her and guard her until he says the word."

We continued the online investigation, scanning through so many articles about corporate buyouts and stock options that my eyes started to cross.

"It's weird that there's no hint of anything shady in Granger's past in anything we've read so far," Bess commented as we read an article from a back issue of a national business journal. "I mean, a lot of those big financial guys get in trouble somewhere along the line, but there's not even a hint of anything suspicious about this guy."

George nodded. "Good point," she said. "Maybe it's time to dig a little deeper. . . ."

I winced. Whenever George gets that particular gleam in her eyes, it means she's about to do something illegal, or at least highly irregular. She can hack through any ordinary firewall like it's nothing, and takes trickier ones as an exciting challenge. Normally I try to discourage that sort of behavior as much as possible; as a lawyer's daughter, lawbreaking of any sort always troubles me. However, I figured that in this case, whatever we might find out would make it worth looking the other way for a while. I didn't say a word as she started typing rapidly.

Despite her best efforts, though, George didn't come up with anything dastardly or even slightly despicable in Granger's past. "He's clean," she said, sounding slightly annoyed at the fact. "I'd put money on it."

Coming from George, that was practically an iron-clad guarantee. I stood and stretched my shoulders. "Well, I guess that's good news," I said. "If this is Granger's first criminal act, it probably means Leslie's less likely to get hurt."

George glanced at me, looking grim. "Or maybe it means he's so desperate for the mayor's job that he's willing to do *anything*."

• • • •

"How about a portable CD player?" Mrs. Fayne said. "Or a nice new set of barbecue tools?"

"Neither of those seem quite right," I said. "But keep the good ideas coming! I need all the help I can get, or you're all going to see a very embarrassed and pathetic daughter at that party on Thursday night."

George's mother chuckled sympathetically. "I'm sure you'll come up with something wonderful, Nancy," she assured me, her brown eyes twinkling.

When George, Bess, and I had emerged from George's room, we found George's parents playing a lively game of cards. They had immediately corralled us and insisted we join them for ice cream. All five of us were now sitting around the table in the Faynes' bright, big country kitchen discussing my gift dilemma.

Mr. Fayne licked some chocolate sauce off his spoon. "Well, if you need any help shopping, I could come along and help you out," he said. "Say, tomorrow night, around seven?"

Mrs. Fayne made a face at him. "Very funny, dear," she said. She glanced at the rest of us. "He's taking me to the recital over at the university tomorrow night," she explained. "He's been trying to get out of it all week—says classical music puts him to sleep."

"At least I should get a good nap out of it," Mr. Fayne joked.

I recalled that George had mentioned something about that earlier. "I hear you're a fan of Leslie Simmons," I remarked, trying to sound casual. "She's supposed to be quite a pianist."

"Oh, she is! She's wonderful," Mrs. Fayne replied enthusiastically. "She just makes the music come alive."

After our dessert break, my friends and I excused ourselves while George's parents returned to their card game. I led the way outside.

"Look," I said. "I just realized—by this time tomorrow night, a whole lot more people are going to know that Leslie isn't around when she doesn't show for that recital."

"*If* she doesn't show," George corrected.

"Okay—*if,*" I agreed. "In the meantime, I think we should keep investigating. Let's drive over to Morris Granger's place and see if we can turn up anything interesting there. Maybe we'll find some clues—or even Leslie herself!" I was feeling a growing sense of urgency about the case. Not only was Leslie's disappearance going to be harder and harder for her parents to hide, but I had just realized that I had promised to spend the next afternoon and all day Wednesday helping out with a charity tag sale. This could be my last chance to crack the case.

"Are you sure it's such a good idea to go to his house?" Bess said dubiously. "Seems pretty risky to me. What if he catches us snooping around?"

George sighed. "Give it up, Bess," she advised. "You know she's going anyway. We might as well tag along and try to keep her out of trouble."

I grinned. "Come on," I said. "I'll drive."

At that, Bess looked more dubious than ever. "Are you sure?" she said. "I don't mind driving. Really. And my car is much closer than yours."

She pointed to her car, which was parked exactly one space closer on the curb than mine. I rolled my eyes. For some reason Bess doesn't trust me behind the wheel. It's not that I'm an unsafe driver—I always follow the speed limit, and rarely forget to signal before I make a turn. However, I have occasionally been known to get slightly distracted when I'm thinking about a case, and this means I'll forget to check the gas gauge and run out of gas. Or I might leave the door open when I leave the car and thus run down the battery. Or forget to take the key out of the ignition and accidentally lock it inside the car.

Of course, that sort of thing almost never happens. Probably no more than once a month or so. Still, Bess just doesn't trust me.

She made a big show of carefully checking the gas

gauge as she climbed into the passenger seat. "We're good," she told George. "There's about half a tank. That should be enough to get us to the other side of town and back, even with Nancy driving."

"Ha-ha," I said with a snort. "Come on, let's get those seat belts on so we can get moving. It's getting late."

It didn't take us long to find Granger's home. It was located in a luxurious new town house community on the outskirts of River Heights. We knew the address from George's snooping earlier. To avoid suspicion, I carefully parked a few doors down.

We climbed out of the car. There were no regular streetlights in the development, but tastefully landscaped lighting fixtures made it easy to get a clear look around. Granger's town house was an end unit. It was two stories high in the front, but from where we were standing we could see that the neatly mowed lawn dropped off sharply in the back. The house most likely featured a walk-out basement with a nice view of the small lake behind. A large white van bearing the words TAYLOR'S TIRELESS CLEANING SERVICE was parked right in front. As we watched, several apron-clad women hurried up the front steps carrying various cleaning implements. The front door was propped open with a metal dustpan.

"Looks like the cleaning service is here," George

said, checking her watch. "Weird time for them to be working."

"I guess they work around Granger's schedule," Bess suggested. "My mom has hired Taylor's Cleaning Service before, and that's sort of their specialty—they have people available twenty-four hours a day. They'll come and vacuum your house at midnight if you want. Granger probably arranged for them to come tonight because he's out of town or at a business dinner or something."

"Makes sense, I guess." George shrugged. "That means this was a wasted trip though. Granger's not here to spy on, and now we won't even be able to get a close look at his house with all these cleaners hanging around."

"Don't be so sure," I said. "Look, the front door is wide open."

Bess looked shocked. "You can't just walk in there, Nancy!"

I grinned at her. "Watch me."

Despite my confident words, my heart was pounding as I took a step toward the front door. I felt George grab my arm.

"Wait," she said. "This is a bad idea. What if you get caught? Or what if Granger comes home while you're in there?"

"Hmm, good point," I said. My friends looked

relieved. "Keep a lookout for Granger," I continued. "I'll come up with something to tell the cleaners if they catch me."

My friends' expressions returned to dismay as I hurried toward Granger's town house. I waited until none of the cleaning people were in sight. Then I dashed up the steps and into the house. My heart was thumping in my chest. I knew my father would disapprove if he was there. But he wasn't there, I told myself, glancing around the art-lined front hall and darting into the nearest room. Besides, I didn't have time to worry about following the rules—not if Leslie was in as much trouble as I thought she was.

The room I'd just entered seemed to be some sort of sitting room. It had a carpeted floor, elegant drapes, and expensive-looking furniture. Stepping toward the front window, I pulled aside the heavy curtain and peeked outside. Bess and George were still standing on the sidewalk where I'd left them— but they were no longer alone. Several young men had joined them, and I could see them jostling each other in their eagerness to talk to Bess.

I rolled my eyes. George and I like to joke that Bess could meet a cute guy in a nunnery, and sometimes I almost think it's true. Guys are drawn to her like paperclips to a magnet. Her all-American good looks and curvy figure have something to do with that, of course. But I think her bubbly personality has even more to do with it. She has a way of smiling and listening that makes whoever she's talking to at the moment feel like the most important person in the world.

Of course, Bess's winning personality wasn't much help to me at the moment. At least George still seemed to be keeping an eye on the incoming road.

That reminded me—I might not have much time. It was getting late. Unless he was out of town, Granger would certainly be home before too much longer. I had to work fast.

I listened at the door until I was pretty sure none of the cleaning people were in the hallway. Fortunately it sounded like most of them were either upstairs or in the kitchen at the back of the house. Taking a deep breath, I dashed across the hall to the next door. I listened briefly, but heard nothing on the other side. When I opened it, I saw steps leading down into darkness.

"Basement," I whispered, moving on to the next door.

This time I struck gold. I could tell right away that the new room was Granger's home office. A large, leather-topped desk dominated the space. Several versions of a Granger for Mayor campaign poster were tacked up on a corkboard with notes scribbled here and there. A large set of metal filing cabinets lined one wall, and bookshelves filled with volumes of boring-looking financial and business texts filled another.

I smiled. If Granger was up to something fishy, surely I would find evidence of it here.

I didn't waste any time getting started on my snooping. Sitting down in the black-leather chair behind the desk, I sifted through the piles of papers, looking for anything suspicious. Everything seemed to be in order there, so I turned to the first filing cabinet. I opened it and glanced at the tightly packed papers inside.

That was all I had time for before I heard a terrible sound: a dog barking. And it sounded like it was coming from inside the house.

"Shoot," I muttered to myself. "Either a neighbor's dog just wandered in through that open door, or . . ."

"Hello, Ms. Taylor!" A man's voice rang out from somewhere nearby. It was slightly muffled, as if drifting in from outside. "Sorry to interrupt your work, but my dinner ended earlier than expected."

My heart pounded. Unless I missed my guess, Morris Granger was home—and that meant it was time for me to get out of there!

I cracked open the office door and peered out. There was no one in the hallway. Maybe I still had time to escape. I carefully stepped out. Suddenly, a small white blur flew through the air toward me. The dog. I'd already forgotten about the dog!

Sure enough, the blur slowed and turned into a small white dog that started yapping excitedly, bouncing up and down and scrabbling at my legs. It seemed friendly enough, but it was definitely making a racket. I did my best to dodge around it, still hoping to slip out the door while Granger talked to the cleaning people.

"What is it, Fluffy?" the man's voice boomed, sounding much closer this time. Footsteps sounded on the front stoop just outside.

I froze. Glancing around, I gauged the distance to the kitchen. But some of the cleaning people were probably still in there. If I ran upstairs, I would be trapped. I could try to make it to that front room—it probably wasn't used much, and I might be able to climb out the window. But my split second of hesitation had already cost me too much time. Any moment now Granger would reach the front door, step inside, and see me. I had to get out of sight any way I could.

Gently shoving away the excited little dog with my foot, I leaped across the hall and yanked open the basement door. I slipped through and pulled the door shut behind me just as I heard footsteps clump onto the wooden floorboards in the hallway.

"What's the matter, Fluffy?" Granger's voice came again, only slightly muffled this time by the thin wood of the basement door. "Are you barking at those monsters in the basement again?"

I sidled down the stairs in case he opened the door, feeling my way as best I could in the darkness. To my surprise, the basement was a little lighter at the bottom. I glanced over and saw a large sliding glass door on the back wall.

Of course! I thought with a quick flash of hope. The yard dropped off in the back—a walk-out basement. I could slip out, and nobody would ever know I was in there. . . .

Hurrying over to the door, I pulled at the handle. But even after fiddling with the lock, trying it in every position, the door didn't budge. I yanked at it in frustration, wondering if it was stuck.

Then, as I squinted desperately at the door handle, I saw my answer: A solid metal padlock was hanging from the handle on the other side of the glass, locking the door from the outside. I clenched my fist and pounded the glass in frustration. How was I going to get out now? Even if I hid out in the basement until Granger went to bed, I was sure he had some kind of security system.

I froze, realizing I might not have to worry about that. I'd just heard the basement door swing open. A second later Fluffy was dancing around my feet again.

"You may be right about the monster this time, Fluffy." Granger's jovial voice drifted down from the top of the stairs. "I heard it that time too. Hope those darn squirrels didn't find a way back in."

A second later an overhead light flickered on. I could now see that the basement was nothing more than a moderately sized, nearly empty room holding little more than the furnace and water heater. I heard a footstep on the stairs, and then another. Granger was coming down. There was nowhere to hide, and the door was locked.

I was trapped!

5

Close Calls

I **almost moaned out** loud in my panic, wondering if I could possibly squeeze out of sight behind the water heater. Then, suddenly, I noticed movement on the outside of the sliding glass door.

"Bess!" I hissed under my breath, recognizing my friend's bright blond hair.

I glanced toward the stairs. There was paneling covering part of the stairwell, which meant Granger's legs wouldn't be visible until he was about halfway down. It also meant he wouldn't be able to see me until he was almost at the bottom of the stairs.

Fluffy had left my feet and raced back up the stairs and out of my sight, still barking excitedly. "All right, all right." Granger laughed. "Come on, let's see what you're so interested in down here, little guy."

I cast a frantic glance outside. Bess was working away at the lock—she has a knack for anything mechanical, and I knew it was only a matter of time before she cracked the lock and got the door open. Unfortunately time was the one thing we *didn't* have.

Footsteps. Granger was moving. I watched nervously as an expensive-looking black dress shoe and dark trouser leg stepped into view, soon followed by another. At least he was taking the steps incredibly slowly. . . .

Bess was still working, but time was running out. I took a deep breath, trying to figure out what to say when Granger saw me. Maybe I could still talk my way out of this.

At that moment, over the noise of Fluffy's barking, I heard a wonderful sound: a ringing phone. Granger muttered something under his breath, sounding annoyed.

"Come on, Fluffy," he called. "Get up here. I'd better see who that is. I'll check out your monster in a minute."

The footsteps hurried up the stairs and were followed by the dog's clicking toenails. I finally exhaled, almost passing out from relief.

I peered outside again. Bess was still working at the lock, her expression focused and grim. Suddenly a tiny beam of light appeared right behind her.

Squinting past it, I saw George's face bending closer, holding the light on the lock so Bess could see better. I recognized the penlight George had bought at Riverside Electronics. She always told us that thing would come in handy someday.

The light seemed to help. Within seconds Bess was yanking the lock off the door handle. A moment later she and George slid open the glass door.

"Thank goodness!" I gasped, rushing out immediately and grabbing them both in a big hug. "I thought I was dead meat when I saw that lock. How did you know where I was?"

George glanced in through the glass door. "We'll tell you in a minute," she said. "Come on. I think he's coming back."

Sure enough, I turned just in time to see Fluffy leaping down the last few steps. The little dog let out a flurry of barks and raced toward the door.

"Yikes!" I exclaimed, jumping forward and sliding the door shut just in time. The dog leaped up and hit it with his front paws, whining with frustration.

We didn't wait around to see if his master was coming down behind him. Bess quickly snapped the padlock back into place. Then, following the thin beam of George's penlight, we raced around the side of the house toward my car.

• • • •

By the time I got home it was very late, and I was feeling frustrated. I still hadn't found out anything useful about Granger, even after taking such a big risk and almost getting busted.

It was a good thing George got sick of watching Bess flirt with those guys and went to look around the yard. If Granger had caught me down there . . .

I shuddered, not bothering to finish the thought. Obviously luck had been with me that night. I found out later that George had been wandering around in the yard on the side of the house when Granger arrived home. She'd ducked around the back of the house and glanced in the basement door just in time to see me come downstairs and try the door. Realizing my dilemma, she'd raced back out front to grab Bess, who immediately grabbed her deluxe Swiss Army knife from her purse and ran to my aid. It had taken George a few minutes to convince her cousin's suitors to scram, but then she'd hurried back to help Bess.

The light was on in my father's home office when I let myself into the house. I glanced in and saw him at his desk, leaning over some paperwork.

"Hi, Dad," I greeted him.

He jumped, clearly startled by my appearance in the doorway. "Oh! Nancy," he said, looking at his watch. "There you are. Did you have fun with your friends?"

"Sure," I said.

I couldn't help notice that he looked tired and worried. He always worked hard, but that usually just seemed to energize him. I suspected that what Heather and Clay Simmons had told him was weighing heavily on his mind. He was so honest and upstanding by nature, I was sure that keeping something so important from the police was making him feel extremely conflicted.

What a way to spend his birthday week, I thought. That made me feel a flash of guilt. In all the excitement over the Simmons case, I hadn't devoted any time to coming up with a great idea for a gift.

I said good night and headed upstairs, though I wasn't really tired. My mind was still ticking away, trying to come up with a new approach to the case. I briefly considered going to see Mr. and Mrs. Simmons myself and trying to convince them to tell me what they knew. But I was afraid they would suspect that Dad had told me about Leslie's disappearance, and I didn't want to compromise their trust in him. I would have to figure out another way.

If only I could find out more about Granger somehow—find out if he was really making designs on Rackham Industries, and what he'd done about it so far. Maybe that could provide a clue that would help us find Leslie.

Checking my watch, I wondered if it was too late to call Ned. His classes at the university didn't start for a couple of weeks, but he was still working part-time at the *Bugle*. Deciding to risk waking him, I called his cell phone, so as not to disturb the rest of his family.

He picked up after a couple of rings. "Hello?"

"Hi, it's me," I said.

I could almost hear his smile through the phone. "Hey," he said, sounding very much awake. "How are you doing, me?"

"Fine," I said quickly. "Listen, what do you have planned for tomorrow? Do you have to work?"

"Not until after lunch," Ned said. "Why? What do you have in mind?"

I took a deep breath, realizing that I hadn't spoken to him since I'd uncovered my new mystery. "Well, it's sort of a long story," I began. "But I just had an idea. . . ."

The next day Ned picked me up after breakfast.

"Did you set it up?" I asked as I climbed into the passenger seat of his car.

He slid into the driver's seat and glanced over at me. "Yep," he replied. "Called first thing this morning. I'm due at the office at nine thirty. We should be right on time."

59

I smiled, relieved. "Great."

So far my new plan was working out perfectly. I crossed my fingers, hoping that the rest would go as well. I'd asked Ned to set up an interview with the CEO of Rackham Industries, claiming that he was researching an article about local businesses. Since Mr. Nickerson owned the *Bugle* and Ned had been writing for the paper all summer, there was no reason why Ned writing the article wouldn't be plausible.

"I just hope they aren't too surprised when you show up with me," Ned said. "I told them I was bringing an assistant. Chances are he's going to recognize you, you know."

I nodded, knowing that was a chance I had to take. One of the side effects of my amateur sleuthing is that I've become sort of well known around town. My picture has been in the paper more than anyone's except maybe the mayor's, and people I hardly know sometimes stop me on the street to ask if I'm working on any interesting mysteries at the moment.

"We'll figure something out," I told Ned as he pulled away from the curb. "I really want to be there when you talk to him. If something fishy is going on between Granger and Rackham Industries, he might let something slip."

I checked my watch, making a mental note to

keep track of the time. I was supposed to check in for my charity duties at noon. That didn't give me much time.

"So what are you going to do with this info if you get it?" Ned asked.

"I'm not sure," I admitted. "I guess it depends on what we find out. If it's juicy enough, it might be time to hand over the case to the police and let them take care of the rest."

I still wasn't sure that was a safe option as long as Leslie was still missing. The more I thought about the case, the more serious it seemed. Deadly serious.

"Maybe I'll talk to Dad first," I said. "My gut tells me he already knows about the case—and he probably knows whether there's a ransom note and what it says and everything. I'm sure he can help me figure out what to do."

Ned nodded. "I wouldn't worry too much about it yet, anyway," he said. "You don't want to count your clues until they're hatched. Or found. Or something."

I knew he was trying to make me feel better, but somehow his words made me more anxious than ever.

A few minutes later we entered the Rackham Industries headquarters—a large glass office building in the heart of downtown River Heights. The security guard at the front desk directed us to the CEO's suite on the top floor. "Just take the elevator all the way up," the guard said. "There'll be someone at reception up there to buzz you in."

When we stepped out of the elevator, though, there was no one in sight behind the clear glass doors at the end of the elevator bank. Ned tried one of the handles, but the door was locked.

I pointed to a little device on the wall beside the doors. "Looks like you need a card key to get into this floor," I said. "Or someone at the desk has to buzz you in, like the guard said."

"Weird." Ned glanced at his watch. "We're right on schedule. They know we're coming. So where is everybody?"

I looked around. Through the glass doors, it was easy to see that there was no one seated behind the large, crescent-shaped reception desk. Beyond the desk there was a small waiting area, and behind that, a large door with a brass nameplate reading JACK HALLORAN, CHIEF EXECUTIVE OFFICER, RACKHAM INDUSTRIES.

"Maybe we should pound on the glass until Halloran hears us and comes to let us in himself," Ned joked.

I smiled. "Too bad Bess isn't here—she could just

pick the lock," I said, remembering her performance the night before.

"Probably not," Ned corrected. "These sorts of security systems are all electronic nowadays. We need George for this kind of thing."

Just then, an attractive, middle-aged woman came into view on the other side of the doors. She spotted us immediately, let out a gasp, and hurried to push open the glass doors.

"I'm so sorry!" she exclaimed, sounding a little flustered. "I had no idea. . . . You must be Mr. Halloran's nine thirty appointment. I hope you weren't waiting long?"

"It's okay," Ned replied politely. "No big deal."

The secretary shook her head. "Well, I'm so sorry," she said. "I just stepped away from the desk for a moment." She glanced at the desk, seeming perturbed. "Irresponsible brat of an intern," she muttered under her breath, so quietly that I almost didn't catch it.

Then she turned back to us with a brilliant, professional smile. She invited us to take a seat in the waiting area while she let the CEO know that we were there.

A moment later she ushered us into the CEO's office. Mr. Halloran was a tall, burly man with a quick smile and a hearty laugh. He shook Ned's hand and then mine, seeming unperturbed by my unexpected presence.

"You're Carson Drew's girl, aren't you?" he asked. When I nodded, he grinned. "Good man, that Carson. Plays a mean game of golf, too."

"Yes, he loves the game," I said politely. "I hope you don't mind my tagging along. I'm thinking of taking some journalism classes, and Ned offered to show me the ropes a little."

"No problem." Mr. Halloran sat down at his desk, leaning back in his chair with his hands behind his head. "Ask away, you two."

So much for my hopes of being incognito, I thought while Ned pulled out his mini–tape recorder and a notebook. I only hoped that my reputation as a detective wouldn't make Halloran too cautious about what he said.

The interview began. Mr. Halloran answered all of Ned's questions easily, without a hint of hesitation or concern. He seemed a little surprised when I blurted out a few questions of my own, but answered those as well. I asked him about Granger and his possible plans for Rackham Industries. Halloran merely shrugged off all such issues as rumors.

Finally, as Ned started thanking Halloran for his

time, I blurted out one last question in desperation. "Mr. Halloran," I said, "do you know Leslie Simmons?"

The CEO looked surprised by the sudden change of topic, but he nodded. "As a matter of fact, I do," he said. "I've known her parents for years, and I've heard young Leslie play the piano many times. I'm a big fan of classical music, and of talented new musicians—especially local ones. Did you know that Rackham Industries is sponsoring that young musician's scholarship to the conservatory?"

As a matter of fact, I hadn't known that. It was an interesting twist, but did it mean anything? Ned and I listened politely as Halloran rambled on about his music collection for a minute or two, then wrapped up the interview. I was ready to admit that it seemed to be a big dead end. I was willing to bet that Halloran had no inkling of any plot having to do with Granger or the Simmonses. But was that because it didn't exist, or was Granger just even more clever than I thought?

I was musing over that thought as Ned and I stepped through Halloran's office door into the reception area. The sound of the secretary's irritated voice met us. She seemed to be scolding someone.

Glancing at the desk, I saw a pretty, dark-haired

girl about my age sitting in one of the chairs. She had a pout on her face and was rolling her eyes as the secretary continued to chide her.

"Deirdre Shannon!" I blurted out in shock.

6

Advances and Retreats

Sure enough, the girl behind the desk was Deirdre Shannon, the richest, snobbiest girl in town. Just our luck.

"What are you doing here?" she and I said to each other at the same time.

She scowled at me. Then she noticed Ned, and her expression played through an interesting range of emotions—from surprise to delight to embarrassment.

I hid a smile. Deirdre had always taken great pride in her family's wealth, never hesitating to show off her expensive car or the latest fashions. It had to be mortifying for her to be caught working like a regular person—especially by someone she couldn't stand, which would be me. Deirdre and I had known each other for years and years, but even back in kindergarten we'd mixed about as well as oil and water.

As usual Deirdre hid whatever vulnerability she might be feeling by going on the offensive. "What are you snooping around here for?" she demanded, glaring at me.

"Deirdre!" The secretary sounded shocked. "Miss Drew and Mr. Nickerson had an appointment with Mr. Halloran. There's no need to be rude to them."

Deirdre tossed her dark hair behind her shoulder. "You don't know nosy Nancy. She's always up to something—like spying on me, for instance." She turned and smiled coquettishly at my boyfriend. "Of course, it's always cool to see you, Ned, no matter what the reason."

Ned shot me an amused glance. He knows that Deirdre's huge, ongoing crush on him is a constant source of entertainment for me and my friends.

"Thanks, Deirdre," he said pleasantly. "So what *are* you doing here, anyway?"

Deirdre shrugged, and annoyance—or maybe embarrassment—creased her brow once again. "Oh, my parents are friends with Halloran from the country club," she said. "For some reason, they thought it would be a good idea for me to try an internship here this summer. It's a totally lame idea, you know? I tried to talk them out of it, but . . ."

She looked so uncomfortable and humiliated that I almost felt sorry for her. For Deirdre, being caught working is probably like anybody else being caught stealing candy from babies. She'd probably never live this down.

"So, Deirdre," I blurted out, my sympathy overcoming my usual distaste for her. "As long as you're here, maybe you can help me out with something. My dad's birthday is this week, and I'm having trouble finding a gift for him. Your father must be almost as hard to shop for as mine—do you have any ideas?"

Deirdre looked startled. "I don't know," she said. "What about a new pair of skis? That's what I got my dad last year."

"Hmm! Good idea," I said, even though I knew my father wasn't particularly interested in skiing. "I'll think about that. Thanks. Come on, Ned—we'd better get going."

A moment later, as the elevator doors slid shut in front of us, Ned glanced at me. "Okay, what was all that about?"

"What?" I asked innocently.

He crossed his arms over his chest and raised his eyebrows. "That," he said succinctly. "Asking Deirdre for advice back there."

"Oh." I grinned and shrugged. "Well, you have to admit, she *does* know a lot about shopping."

• • • •

As Ned drove me to my volunteer project, we talked over what we knew about the case so far. It still wasn't much.

"I'm not sure what to do next," I admitted as Ned stopped at a red light. "No matter what I try, I'm not finding anything I can use. I'm still sure my theory is right, but how am I supposed to prove it?"

Ned shrugged. "Good question. Too bad Halloran was a dead end. If you'd come up with any evidence that Granger was angling to take over Rackham Industries and using the mayor's office to do it, even Chief McGinnis would have to listen to you."

"I know." I frowned, thinking hard. "But how else can I get that kind of evidence? Maybe I should try to talk to Granger himself."

Ned shot me a quick glance before returning his attention to the road. "That doesn't seem like such a great idea," he said. "If Granger really is the kidnapper, you don't want to let him know you're on to him—or *you* might disappear too."

I chewed on my lower lip. "But he wouldn't have to know," I said. "I would just need to be subtle. . . ." Suddenly I sat up straight. "I know. Deirdre!"

"Huh?"

"Deirdre's family belongs to the country club," I

reminded Ned. "So does Granger. And I'm pretty sure the Simmonses do too. If I could finagle an invitation out of Deirdre . . ."

Ned snorted. "Yeah, like that's going to happen," he said. "Seriously, Nancy, you're really not even sure yet that your kidnapping theory is right. Do you really want to put yourself through the Deirdre Experience only to have it turn out that Leslie's just visiting relatives or something?"

I was about to argue, but I sighed instead. I had to admit that he had a point. Hunch or no hunch, I didn't have any solid evidence that there was actually a mystery to be solved.

"I guess you're right," I said heavily. "I just wish I knew for sure where Leslie Simmons is right now."

"I know." Ned sounded sympathetic. "Well, maybe she'll turn up soon and you'll have your answers."

"Her music camp recital is tonight," I said. "If she shows up for that, I guess this will all be a big false alarm. If she doesn't . . ." I glanced at Ned. "Hey, want to go to the recital with me? It's open to the public—George's parents are going."

Ned shrugged. "Sure, I guess."

"From what I know about Leslie, she wouldn't miss that for anything," I mused, talking more to myself than to Ned. "If she turns up, it means there's no

71

mystery, and we'll just have an evening of nice music. If she doesn't, it will prove that something fishy really *is* going on." Seeing Ned shoot me a slightly doubtful look, I added, "For me, at least."

I realized it might also give me an opportunity to talk to some of Leslie's friends and teachers. One of them might know something useful.

There was no more time to think about it just then. Ned pulled his car up to the university's football stadium, where my charity group was setting up for a giant fund-raising tag sale. The sale was scheduled to begin the next day and run through the weekend, and was expected to attract thousands of visitors. All sorts of local businesses had donated items or services to be sold or raffled off, and many individuals had contributed as well. I had volunteered to work at the setup and also help run one of the booths the next day.

After asking Ned to call Bess and George to see if they would come to the recital too, I hopped out of the car, and Ned drove away. Then I sighed and walked into the stadium, feeling a little impatient at the thought of missing out on a whole afternoon of investigating.

I tried to look on the bright side as I glanced around at the tables piled full of countless donated items, from outgrown tricycles to valuable antique vases and everything in between. I probably wouldn't be able to do much sleuthing while I was here—but maybe I'd at least be able to find something for Dad's birthday.

"So did you find anything for your father?" Bess asked as Ned pulled into a parking space in one of the university lots that evening. She and George were sitting in the backseat, and I was in the passenger seat up front.

"No," I said. "I must've checked out every table in the place. I had the perfect excuse for browsing: I was in charge of one of the pricing guns. But I didn't find anything good."

I sighed, feeling another pang of guilt about not spending more time shopping. Still, I knew that Dad would understand if he knew what was going on. He knows that I can't resist a mystery, especially one where someone might be in real trouble. And he knows that I can't think about much else until it's solved.

My friends and I found the hall where the recital was being held. I checked my watch as Ned bought tickets in the high-ceilinged, carpeted lobby.

"We have about half an hour until it's supposed to start," I told Bess and George. "That should give us time to find out whether Leslie is here—and start asking questions if she isn't."

"Yoo-hoo! Girls!"

I looked up to see George's parents hurrying toward us through the crowd that was beginning to trickle into the auditorium. Mrs. Fayne was waving and smiling. Mr. Fayne looked slightly disgruntled.

"You didn't mention that you and your friends would be here tonight, Georgia," Mr. Fayne said. "If I'd known, I would've made you bring your mother so I could stay home and watch the game on TV."

"Oh, stop it." Mrs. Fayne gave her husband a playful shove.

George wrinkled her nose at her hated full name. Her parents were just about the only people who could call her Georgia and get away with it.

"It was kind of a last-minute plan," she said.

"Well, I hope you're not too disappointed," Mrs. Fayne said, shaking her head. "I just heard that Leslie Simmons won't be playing tonight after all. The whole place is buzzing about it."

"Really?" I perked up. "Are you sure?"

Mrs. Fayne nodded. "I ran into some women I know from my bridge club. They told me they heard it straight from Leslie's music teacher, Mrs. Diver. Such a disappointment."

Ned returned at that moment from the ticket window. He exchanged greetings and pleasantries with George's parents. A moment later, the Faynes spotted some other friends and excused themselves.

"Okay, now what?" George said as soon as they were gone. "We know Leslie's not here. So what are we supposed to do now?"

"Let's split up," I suggested. "We can all talk to people, try to find out if anyone knows anything. Oh, and let me know if you find that music teacher, Mrs. Diver. I'd like to talk to her."

My friends nodded, and we went our separate ways. I headed into the large, airy auditorium. A few dozen people were already inside. Some were in their seats reading their programs, while others stood chatting near the doors, or in clusters near the stage, watching the students set up their music stands and instruments on stage.

I wandered down the aisle, pretending to watch the students, but I was actually paying more attention to the conversations going on nearby. I heard several older women chatting about Leslie's absence and expressing kind concern as they discussed the possible reasons. A little farther down the aisle, a pair of women in their late twenties were debating about whether to stay or go, since they'd come primarily to hear Leslie. Mrs. Fayne was right. Everyone here was talking about Leslie.

I glanced toward the stage. A short, plump woman had just scurried out onto the stage with a skinny teenage boy in tow. The woman had curly bright-red hair, and was wearing a flowered dress and cat's-eye glasses on a chain around her neck. The boy had pimples on his nose and a miserable expression on his face. As I watched, the woman led the way to the grand piano at one side of the stage and lifted the cover off the keys. She gestured at the keyboard and I could see her chattering rapidly at the boy, though I couldn't quite hear her words from where I was standing. I took a few steps forward, straining to hear.

"It's a shame, isn't it?" a woman's voice said from very nearby.

I jumped, realizing that I'd just stepped in front of a preppy-looking woman in her early forties. She was perched on the arm of one of the aisle seats, watching the stage. She nodded toward the woman and teenager.

"Poor Matthew has to step in and play Leslie's part," the woman said. "He must be terribly nervous."

I smiled politely. "Yes, I just heard that Leslie won't be here tonight," I said. "I was really looking forward to hearing her play. Do you know why she can't make it? Is she sick or something?"

"Oh, no, nothing like that," the woman replied. "She has an audition on Thursday morning for the conservatory scholarship and she's on retreat for a few days, getting in some extra practice."

"It sounds like you know Leslie well," I commented, carefully keeping my voice casual. Had I just found the answer to the mystery? "My name's Nancy, by the way. Nancy Drew."

"I'm Marcia Sharon," the woman said, not seeming to recognize my name as she shook my hand. "And yes, I know Leslie. My eldest daughter, Diane, is a classmate of hers at school, and the two of them are in music camp together this summer. My Diane plays the cello. Mrs. Diver says she's the most talented cellist she's seen in years." The woman's eyes reflected her pride in her daughter.

"How nice," I said politely.

I was about to question her further when George suddenly appeared at my side. "Excuse me," George said breathlessly, grabbing my arm. "I'm afraid Nancy is needed elsewhere."

Before I could protest, she dragged me halfway down the aisle. "What was that about?" I asked, yanking my arm back and glancing at Mrs. Sharon, who was already talking to someone else. "I was just finding out some useful information."

"I thought you wanted us to let you know if we found Leslie's music teacher," George said. She pointed to the stage. "Well, that's her up there by the piano, talking to that skinny kid."

"Oh." I rubbed my arm absently as I glanced at the woman in the flowered dress. I sighed. "Well, it might not matter after all. That woman I was talking to back there—Mrs. Sharon—says Leslie's on a retreat to practice for her audition."

"Sharon?" George said. "Did you say Mrs. Sharon?"

"Yes. Why?"

"Wasn't that the name we saw on the list of audition times for the scholarship contest?" George prompted. "We thought it was funny because 'D. Sharon' was so close to 'D. Shannon,' remember?"

"Oh, yeah." I nodded. "She just said her daughter's name is Diane. I guess that means she's trying out for the scholarship too. Mrs. Sharon said she's a cellist."

I glanced at the stage, wondering which of the teens milling around up there was Mrs. Sharon's daughter. I didn't see any cellos up there. Maybe she wasn't set up yet. Or maybe she was skipping the recital to practice for the audition too. . . .

But I wasn't really thinking too hard about Diane Sharon. I was much more interested in what I'd just learned about Leslie Simmons. Could it be true? All this time, was Leslie merely off practicing somewhere, preparing her piece for the scholarship tryouts? Was the mystery only in my head after all?

There could have been other explanations for that scene I saw on the street the day before. Mr. and Mrs. Simmons could have been arguing about almost anything. Just because they looked in the general direction of the police station once or twice didn't necessarily mean anything. Maybe they were fighting about her running for mayor. Or about how to pay for Leslie's tuition at the conservatory if she didn't win the scholarship. Or what to have for dinner even.

I suddenly noticed that George was no longer at my side. Glancing around, I saw that she had hopped up onstage and was talking to Mrs. Diver, pointing to me at the same time. A moment later the two of them hurried in my direction.

Putting a polite smile on my face, I waited for them to climb down off the stage and reach me. I wasn't anywhere near as interested in talking to the music teacher as I had been a few minutes earlier. I figured, however, that it wouldn't hurt to confirm what Mrs. Sharon had told me.

"Hello, Mrs. Diver," I said when George introduced us, shaking the woman's hand. "It's so nice to meet you. My friends and I are really looking forward to hearing your students play tonight. But we were a little disappointed to learn that Leslie Simmons won't be among them!"

The woman's pleasant expression turned into a frown. "Ah, yes," she said in a light, fluttery voice. "I was disappointed by that myself. It hasn't been easy to find someone to take over her part at the last minute."

"You mean you didn't know she was going to be away?" I asked.

"I'm afraid not," Mrs. Diver said. "Her father called me at home over the weekend to let me know she would be going on retreat this week to rehearse." She shook her head, her frown deepening. "I tried to change his mind, of course—even started to offer to help her rehearse myself, stay late after camp or whatnot. But he cut me off before I could finish my sentence." She sounded a bit wounded. "You know, until then I'd always found Clay Simmons a delightful man—polite and witty. But he was a whole different person on the phone that night. Very brusque." She drew herself up to her full height of about five foot even, glowering at the memory. "He all but came out and told me to mind my own business!"

7

Stakeout

George and I made sympathetic noises as Mrs. Diver muttered a bit more about Clay Simmons. All the while my mind was racing. This changed everything. It now looked like there was a mystery to solve here after all!

I was sure this was an important clue. Clay Simmons wasn't the type of person to be rude for no reason—I was certain of that.

He and Heather might have been using this rehearsal-retreat story as a cover, so people wouldn't start asking too many questions about where Leslie was. That way they could keep the kidnapper happy in the hope that he'd return their daughter unharmed.

It occurred to me that I might be exaggerating the meager evidence I had and convincing myself that there was a mystery when there really wasn't one. But I quickly shrugged off the thought. What was the worst that could come of continuing to investigate? If Leslie turned up at that audition on Thursday morning, safe and sound, I would be more than happy to admit that I was wrong and take all the teasing my friends could dish out. But if she didn't . . .

I shook my head. I had to keep digging . . . just in case. Leslie's safety might depend on it.

Unfortunately I wasn't able to continue my investigation until late the following afternoon. By the time the recital let out, it was time to head home to bed. Wednesday morning and early afternoon were filled with the charity tag sale, where I was kept busy marking prices, ringing up sales, and assisting customers.

I finally managed to escape from the sale at around four thirty. Earlier I had called Bess and George and asked them to meet me at Food for Thought, a sandwich shop near the university. I'd called Ned too, but he wasn't home.

After a quick walk across campus, I hurried into the cramped but cheerful shop, which always smelled of sour pickles and frying bacon. My mind was racing as I tried to figure out what to do next. There wasn't much time left; the filing deadline was just a little over forty-eight hours away. If I didn't find Leslie soon, Granger was going to get away with his plan. And I *definitely* didn't want that to happen.

Bess and George were sitting at one of the round, marble-topped tables near the counter. They looked up and waved when they saw me come in.

"Hi," I greeted them. "Glad you're here."

George checked her watch. "We've been here for ten minutes," she said grumpily, "and we're starving. If you hadn't shown up soon, I was going to order without you."

I smiled. "Okay, let's eat," I said. "But get your sandwiches to go, okay? We're short on time, and I want to get going on this investigation."

"Get going?" Bess said. "Get going where? What do you have in mind, Nancy?"

I shrugged. "I'm not sure yet. I have a couple of ideas, but I've hardly had a second all day to think about them."

"Go ahead and think," George said, her gaze wandering to the large menu board above the counter. "Meanwhile, I'll think about ordering a liverwurst and salami with extra cheese."

"Liverwurst?" Bess protested. "Ick! Besides, I thought you said you were in the mood for a burger?"

"Oh, yeah!" George's eyes lit up. She glanced from one side of the menu board to the other, looking conflicted. "They both sound great. Then again, so does the double bratwurst special."

Bess licked her lips. "Ooh, that does sound good. But I'm trying to stay away from the heavy stuff." She patted her belly. "I think I'll have the turkey on rye. . . ."

I tapped my foot impatiently as the cousins continued to debate the menu. I could almost hear the seconds ticking away on the big chrome clock over the shop's door. Was Leslie counting the seconds too, wherever she was? Were her parents counting the seconds until their daughter returned?

As I'd told my friends, I'd been too busy at the tag sale to think much about the case. But now that I had a moment, I realized that I really had no idea how to proceed. I was sure I had the answers in this case— but how could I prove them? If I went to Chief McGinnis and told him what I believed, he would think I was crazy.

I'd have to figure out a way to tie Granger to Leslie's disappearance. I considered trying the fake-interview trick again, but quickly shrugged off that idea. Granger was used to tough business negotiations; a few pointed questions weren't likely to force a confession out of a man like him. Besides, setting up such an interview would probably take too long, especially since I couldn't reach Ned. I chewed my lower lip, trying to come up with other options.

Finally Bess and George made up their minds. We placed our sandwich orders with the short, grizzled old man behind the counter.

"All right, girls," he said in a slow, lightly accented voice. "Have a seat over there if you like. I'll give you a holler when they're ready."

I felt like shouting, "Hurry! Hurry!" as the little man shuffled slowly over to the wooden bin full of rolls behind the counter. His unhurried, deliberate movements seemed to taunt me, to remind me that time was passing and I wasn't making any progress on the mystery. Deciding it was probably better not to drive myself crazy by watching him, I turned and followed my friends back to their table.

"Okay, Nancy," George said as she flopped into a chair. "I can tell you're *really* distracted—otherwise, why would you order a boring sandwich like plain turkey on white? Come on, girl. Condiments were invented for a reason!"

"Sorry, but I don't have time to figure out exciting sandwich combinations right now," I said, carefully keeping my voice low so that the other customers in the shop wouldn't overhear. "I'm too busy thinking about how to prove that Morris Granger kidnapped Leslie."

"You know, I hate to say it, but the more I think about your theory, the more far-fetched it seems," Bess told me, looking troubled. "I mean, I'm not crazy about some outsider coming in and wanting to be mayor of River Heights. Especially someone who might have his eye on Rackham Industries. But I've seen Mr. Granger on TV and stuff, and he really doesn't seem like the criminal type."

"And we didn't find any dirt on him online, remember?" George added. "Why would a guy like him stoop to kidnapping all of a sudden?"

I frowned. "I don't know," I said. "That's why they call it a mystery." I wasn't thrilled about their attitudes. If we were going to help Leslie, we had to act fast, not waste time arguing.

"Why don't you just wait until tomorrow morning and see if she turns up for that audition?" George suggested. "That way, you'll know if there really *is* a mystery."

I shook my head. "That just means wasting another half a day, which Mrs. Simmons could use to fill out that paperwork," I said. "Besides, if Leslie misses her audition, people are *really* going to notice. They were already gossiping about her missing the recital, remember? What if someone gets so worried that they call the police?"

George shrugged. "So what if they do?" she said, playing with a crumpled straw wrapper someone had left on the tabletop. "At the rate the River Heights Police Department moves, they'll get around to investigating sometime next Tuesday."

"Joke about it if you want," I said grimly. "But Leslie could be in deadly danger—and I think we need to do whatever we can to help her."

My friends exchanged a glance. "All right, Nancy," Bess said. "We'll help if we can. But what do you think we should do?"

I took a deep breath. "I think we should tail Granger."

"Oh, yeah," George said sarcastically. "Because that worked so well the last time."

"No, listen," I said. "I'm not talking about going to his house this time. We know where his office is. We can go there right now and wait for him to come out. Then we'll follow him."

"Why?" George asked bluntly.

I shrugged, not wanting to admit that I was feeling a little less than confident about my own plan. "The deadline for the paperwork is getting close," I said. "Granger's probably going to be keeping an eye on Leslie from now on, wherever she is. Maybe he'll lead us there."

Bess's forehead crinkled slightly. "But I thought you said he wouldn't want to have any contact with Leslie—you know, so she couldn't identify him after he lets her go. So what good will it do to follow him?"

"Look," I said, feeling frustrated. Normally I love it when my friends ask intelligent questions about my cases—they help me figure things out. But at the moment, I didn't seem to have any good answers for them. Or for myself. "We need to do *something*. And since Granger is our only suspect, he's also our only lead. Now, are you with me, or not?"

Bess and George glanced at each other. They both shrugged.

"I guess so," George answered for both of them. "I mean, we're not about to let you run off after a possible kidnapper all by yourself."

It wasn't exactly the rousing vote of support I might have hoped for, but it would have to do. "Good," I said.

At that moment the man behind the counter called out our names. Our sandwiches were finally ready. We each grabbed a beverage from the cooler near the counter. After paying for our food, we headed outside.

"Come on," I said. "We'll take my car. That way you guys can eat while I drive."

Bess looked doubtful, but George was already heading for the passenger-side door. "Sounds good to me," she said, reaching into her bag to pull out her sandwich.

We didn't talk much on the short ride to the building where Granger's office was located. My friends were busy eating, and I was busy thinking.

Were they right? I clutched the wheel tightly as I waited for a red light to change. Was this a waste of time?

"Yo!" George mumbled through a mouthful of food. "Earth to Nancy. It's not going to get any greener."

With a start, I realized that the traffic light had changed. I stepped on the gas quickly, causing my car to lurch forward and almost cut off the engine. Bess winced, but kept quiet. I managed to keep us moving, and a moment later I was pulling to the curb directly across from the exit to a parking garage beneath a tall office building.

"So now what?" Bess asked, taking a sip of her jumbo-size soda.

"Now we wait." I cut the engine and leaned back in my seat. "When Granger comes out, we'll follow him."

George looked skeptical. "What if he already left?" she asked. "It's after five o'clock."

"Granger didn't get as rich and successful as he is by cutting out at five every day," I said, trying to sound more confident than I felt. "Don't worry; he's still there."

I reached for my sandwich, ignoring the dubious glances my friends were exchanging.

We sat there in my car and waited. And waited. And then we waited some more.

An hour passed, and then two. All of our sandwiches were long gone. My friends were bored and grumpy, and I was starting to wonder if we were wasting our time. Car after car had emerged from the garage, but Granger hadn't been in any of them.

Finally, just as I checked my watch for the millionth time and saw that it was a little after seven thirty, I caught a flash of movement in the dim interior of the parking garage. A moment later a late-model blue sedan pulled up to the ticket window, and its driver leaned out to hand a pass to the attendant.

I gasped, sitting bolt upright. "That's him!" I said, recognizing the driver immediately. "It's Morris Granger!"

"It's about time," George muttered sourly.

The three of us crouched down in our seats, hiding our faces as the blue sedan pulled out. Granger didn't even glance our way as he drove off down the nearly deserted street.

I threw my car into gear so fast that the engine stalled. "Rats!" I muttered, turning the key to try again.

"Nice driving," Bess commented with a giggle.

Ignoring her, I pulled out and followed Granger's car. There wasn't much traffic for the first couple of blocks and I hung back as far as I dared, not wanting him to notice that he was being tailed. Soon he turned onto busy State Avenue, and I was able to stay a car or two behind him without fear of being sighted.

"What's the point in this, anyway?" George complained. "He's probably just going to drive home, eat dinner, and go to bed. Or something equally thrilling."

I clutched the wheel tighter, knowing that she was probably right. Still, I kept my gaze trained on the taillights of the blue sedan. If he was heading home, he would be making a left soon onto Jackson Street.

And if he did, I was thinking maybe I should just admit that my friends were right and take them home. Driving out to Granger's place again wasn't going to help Leslie any.

My left pinkie finger hovered just over my turn signal, ready to hit it for the turn onto Jackson—but to my surprise, Granger drove right through the intersection without pausing.

"Hey," Bess said. "Shouldn't he have turned back there?"

My heart leaped with sudden hope. Maybe we hadn't wasted the last two and a half hours after all. . . .

"Yep," I said. "*If* he was going home. Which he's obviously not."

George still didn't seem convinced. "All right, so he's going out to eat before he heads home. Big deal."

But instead of turning right to head over to River Street with its bustling shops and lively restaurants, he turned left onto Union Street. I followed.

"Ugh," Bess complained. "Why did he go this way? Everyone knows it's a mess because of the hospital construction work."

Sure enough, the street narrowed quickly into one lane. The construction workers had gone home for the day, but their orange road cones and signs remained.

I slowed the car to a crawl. There was no other traffic in sight, and I didn't want Granger to spot my car and get suspicious. He pulled past the cones and stopped at the curb, then climbed out without glancing around.

"Check it out," I whispered, my heart pounding with excitement. "He's going into the hospital construction site!"

The future site of the Granger Children's Hospital was little more than a maze of support beams with a few temporary plywood walls here and there. Piles of concrete, lumber, and stone sat everywhere, and pale gray plaster dust coated everything, giving the area the look of a moon colony beneath the dim gleam of the setting sun. As we watched, Granger walked right into the heart of the construction site, carefully stepping around the worst of the debris in his business suit and expensive leather shoes.

"What in the world is he doing here at this hour?" George asked in confusion.

I parked haphazardly in the nearest available spot at the curb, almost flattening a road cone in the process. "Don't you get it?" I whispered. "This must be where he's keeping Leslie! It's the perfect place to hide someone!"

Unfortunately it wasn't the perfect place to follow someone, as I soon discovered. My friends and I scurried after our quarry, but it wasn't easy keeping him in sight without being spotted. The support beams weren't large enough to provide much cover, and the debris littering the ground at every step made it difficult to move quietly.

I winced as Bess tripped over a pile of boards, and they fell with a loud clatter. "Ow!" she whispered, grabbing her foot.

"Get down," I hissed, yanking her behind a stack of cement blocks.

George crouched next to us. "Do you think he heard?" she breathed in my ear.

All I could do was shrug. I leaned forward, listening closely for any hint of footsteps moving in our direction. When there was no sound from ahead, I let out a sigh of relief. "I think we're okay," I whispered.

When I peered out from our hiding place, Granger was nowhere to be seen. "Uh-oh," George whispered in my ear. "Looks like we lost him."

"Maybe we should go back," Bess whispered. "He has to come back to his car. Maybe we could just wait, and follow him then."

I glanced at her in disbelief. "Are you kidding?" I whispered. "This could be our big chance to find Leslie! We've got to keep moving."

"I don't know," George put in. "This is getting a little freaky. Maybe one of us should go back to the car and call for help or something, while the others wait here to keep an eye on Granger."

"How can we keep an eye on him when we don't know where he went?" I argued. "Come on, we're wasting time!"

Bess looked skeptical. "I don't know, Nancy," she said. "I think maybe we should—"

She never got to finish her sentence. "Hey!" Morris Granger exclaimed, staring down at us from the top of the cement pile. "What are *you* doing here?"

8

A New Direction

I gulped as Granger clambered down toward us. We were busted!

Bess and George started whispering wildly, desperately concocting any sort of cover story they could come up with. Bess seemed determined to convince Granger that we were just going for a nice evening stroll, while George was attempting some sort of tale about getting a flat tire because of all the construction out on the street. Neither one of them was making much sense.

Granger just gazed at them, looking confused. I decided it was time to try a more direct approach.

"We were following you," I told him boldly. Things had gone far enough. We were out of time— now we needed some real answers. "We know that

97

Leslie Simmons is missing, and we think you might know where she is."

He stared at me. My friends fixed their eyes on me as well, silenced by my audacity. I held my breath, realizing belatedly that my accusation might not have been the wisest move in the world. After all, we were just three ordinary girls, unarmed in a deserted construction site with a man who might possibly be a ruthless kidnapper. . . .

But instead of looking angry, Granger seemed more perplexed than ever. "Leslie Simmons?" he repeated blankly. "Are you telling me that lovely, talented girl who plays the piano so beautifully is . . . missing? As in, gone?"

I hesitated, taken by surprise. "Of course she is," I said. "Um . . ."

"Well, don't just stand there, young lady," Granger exclaimed. "Tell me everything!"

Startled by his unexpected reply, I blurted out the few details I knew—seeing the Simmonses arguing on the street, Leslie's odd absence from the recital, and the rest of it.

Granger listened intently, seeming shocked by each part of the story. "Hmm," he said at last. "But what makes you think she's truly missing, and not just off practicing, as her teacher said?"

I shrugged. "I guess we won't know for sure until

that audition tomorrow morning," I admitted, quickly explaining about the conservatory's scholarship. Again, the man seemed honestly surprised. But was he just a good actor?

Granger grabbed me by the arm. I squeaked, startled by the sudden movement. Beside me, I heard Bess gasp.

"Come on," Granger said urgently, turning and dragging me back in the direction of the street. "We've got to get to the bottom of this right now. I think it's time to talk to the Simmonses."

Soon my friends and I were standing on the Simmonses' front porch as Granger rapped briskly at their door. I snuck a peek at my watch—it was almost nine o'clock.

A moment later the door opened and Clay Simmons stood before us, looking startled.

"Hello," he said, peering at us uncertainly. "Um, can I help you?"

Granger jabbed a thumb in my general direction. "This young lady just informed me that your daughter seems to be missing," he said without preamble. "Is that true?"

Clay gaped at him for a moment, then turned and stared at me. I saw recognition dawn in his eyes. He glanced behind him into the house. "Heather!" he called. "I think you'd better come out here."

Seconds later Heather Simmons appeared at her husband's side. "Why, hello there, Morris, girls," she said uncertainly. "What can I do for you this evening?"

Morris Granger repeated his question. Heather Simmons blinked, but she recovered quickly from her own surprise. "Why don't all of you come inside?"

She led the way into a cozy den off the front hall. A classical recording was playing softly in the background. I wondered idly if it might be Leslie's school orchestra. Soon we were all seated—all except for Granger, who paced restlessly in front of the fireplace.

"Now," he said briskly, "let's get down to business. Miss Drew here seems to think your daughter might be in some trouble—perhaps even kidnapped. If that's true, I want to help however I can. I'd like to put up a ten-thousand-dollar reward for her safe return. Just give me the go-ahead, and I'll make sure the information is plastered all over town by tomorrow morning."

Heather and Clay Simmons appeared a little overwhelmed. "Oh, Morris," Heather said. "We really appreciate such a wonderful, generous offer. But the truth is, we're not even certain that anything is wrong."

I saw her exchange a glance with her husband. Deep worry lines were etched on both their faces. Whether they were certain anything was wrong or not, I could tell they were fearing the worst.

"Please, Mr. and Mrs. Simmons," I spoke up earnestly. "Could you just tell us what's going on? Maybe we could help somehow."

Heather Simmons gave me a slightly suspicious glance. "How did you get involved in this, anyway?" she asked. "Did your father say something to you?"

"No!" I exclaimed immediately, realizing what she was thinking. "I swear, Dad hasn't breathed a word to me. I really figured it out."

Sort of, anyway, I added in my mind, with a guilty peek at Morris Granger. The more time I spent with him, the more certain I was that he didn't have anything to do with Leslie's disappearance.

Meanwhile Heather Simmons sighed and glanced at her husband. "Well," she said after a moment, "we're not even certain that there's anything to worry about. Leslie simply disappeared over the weekend, leaving only a note."

"A note that didn't look like it was written in her handwriting," Clay Simmons broke in with a frown.

His wife nodded. "Yes," she said. "Sort of scribbled though—like she was in a hurry."

"What did the note say?" George asked curiously, beating me to the question.

"Just three words: 'I'll be back,'" Clay replied. "And signed with her name." He shrugged. "At first we assumed she had just gone somewhere for the afternoon. But when she hadn't turned up by dinnertime, and then by bedtime, we naturally started to worry."

"Naturally," Morris Granger said, nodding sympathetically.

Heather smiled at him; then her expression turned anxious again. "We weren't sure what to do," she said. "At first we didn't want to run to the police in case it was just a misunderstanding or something. But when she hadn't turned up by Sunday night—"

"That's when we decided we had to do something," Clay continued. "But by then, the possibility of foul play had crossed our minds. We feared that Leslie might be in greater peril if we went to the police."

"You can say it, Clay," Heather told him with the hint of a smile. "*I* was afraid to go to the police." She glanced around at the rest of us. "My husband wanted to talk to them, especially after we spoke with your father about it, Nancy. He urged us to go straight to Chief McGinnis and tell him everything. But I still thought it was better to wait, in case we heard from the kidnappers, or from Leslie herself.

Now I wonder if we've waited too long. If it's too late." Her voice cracked slightly on the last word. "Who would want to hurt poor Leslie—or our family? And why?"

Morris Granger finally stopped his pacing. He sat down on the couch beside Heather. "It's all right," he said kindly, patting her on the hand. "Hang in there. I'm sure she'll turn up. And my offer stands. I'm a big fan of your daughter's music, and I would be thrilled to play any part in helping you get her back."

"Thank you." This time it was Clay's voice that cracked with emotion.

The classical music was still playing in the background as Mr. and Mrs. Simmons showed us to the door a few minutes later. The melancholy notes of a cello solo reflected my discouraged mood as I bid Mr. and Mrs. Simmons good night and followed my friends out to my car, which was parked behind Granger's sedan at the curb.

Now what? It was pretty clear to me that Mr. Granger was innocent—which meant I'd lost my number-one suspect. No, make that my *only* suspect. We were no closer to finding Leslie than we'd been when this all started. But there had to be a way to solve this. . . . What was I missing?

My friends were quiet as we waved good-bye to Mr. Granger and climbed into my car. It took me two tries to start the engine; I was so deep in thought that I forgot to put the car into gear before stepping on the gas.

"Try to remember how to drive long enough to get us home, okay, Nancy?" George said with a yawn from the backseat. "Oh, and wake me up when we get there."

I caught myself humming a simple melody under my breath as I drove through the quiet, darkened residential streets toward George's house. For a moment I wasn't sure where the tune had come from. Then I realized it was the cello solo I'd just heard playing at the Simmons house.

Suddenly I gasped as an image of a cello flashed in my head. I leaped in my seat, jamming my shoulder against the seat belt and accidentally hitting both the gas and the brake at the same time. The engine let out a loud, protesting *crunch* and cut out, stalling in the middle of the street.

"That's it!" I cried out excitedly. "I've got it!"

9

A New Clue

"What? What's wrong?" Bess yelped.

I grinned at them sheepishly, realizing that they had both been dozing off as I drove. "Sorry," I said, carefully starting the engine again. "Didn't mean to startle you. But listen—I think I know how to find Leslie."

"Really?" George sounded skeptical.

"We've been looking at it all wrong," I explained, pulling over to the curb and putting the car in park so I could talk to them. "This whole time, I've been assuming that someone wanted Leslie to disappear to distract her mother from the mayoral paperwork deadline. But I just realized—it isn't about politics at all. It's about music!"

In the dim glow of the streetlight, Bess looked puzzled. "What do you mean?"

I twisted around to look at George. "Remember that woman I was talking to at the recital?" I asked her. "Mrs. Sharon?"

George shrugged. "Sure," she said. "We joked around about her name. Why?"

"Her daughter Diane is a cello player," I reminded her. "But think about it: There was no cellist playing at the recital, remember?"

"I remember that," Bess said, looking confused. "But who is this Sharon person?"

I quickly explained. "So anyway," I went on, tapping my fingers on the steering wheel, "why wouldn't Diane Sharon be at the recital? Maybe *she* was off practicing for the scholarship auditions too."

"But what does all this mean, Nancy?" George asked with a shrug. "You're not saying that Diane Sharon kidnapped Leslie, are you?"

"Not exactly," I said. "But I think we ought to go talk to her parents and see what they know about all this. Do you have your handheld computer with you, George?"

"Of course." George reached into her bag.

George looked up the Sharons' address on her handheld computer, and I put the car in drive again. Bess still seemed worried.

"But what are we going to say to them?" she said. "It's almost ten P.M.—we can't just go barging in there accusing them of stuff without any proof."

I shrugged. "We'll worry about what to say when we get there," I told her grimly. "If we want Leslie to make it to that audition tomorrow morning at eight fifteen, we've got to act now."

Unfortunately it took us quite a while to find the right house. The Sharons lived at 970 Maplewood Street, but the tiny screen on George's minicomputer had shortened the address, so we spent way too long driving around on Maple Street looking for an address that didn't exist. By the time we finally realized our mistake and found the right street, it was after ten thirty.

Maplewood Street was located in a fancy new subdivision on the outskirts of town, and number 970 turned out to be an opulent home set on an acre of lush grass on a corner lot. When we pulled into the driveway, we saw that there were lights on downstairs.

"At least we won't be waking them up," Bess said.

We climbed out of the car and hurried to the front door. I raised my hand to knock.

"Are you sure this is a good idea?" George asked.

I didn't bother to answer her. Instead I rapped

sharply on the door several times. A moment later a teenage girl opened the door and stared out at us, her jaw moving steadily as she chewed gum.

"Diane?" I asked.

"No," the girl replied, tossing her long, blond ponytail over her shoulder. "I'm Rachel. The baby-sitter."

"Does Diane Sharon live here?" George asked.

Rachel nodded. "Yeah, but she's not home," she said. "That's why I'm here watching Lewis."

"Oh." I swallowed my disappointment. "Do you know where Diane is, or when she'll be home? Or Mr. and Mrs. Sharon?"

The baby-sitter shrugged and snapped her gum. "Nope," she said. She let out a short laugh. "I'm just glad you're not them, 'cause Lewis was supposed to be in bed over an hour ago!"

Just then a small, brown-haired boy appeared in the hallway behind her. He was wearing pajamas and carrying a comic book, and looked about eight years old.

"Hey," he said, sounding sleepy. "What's going on? Are Mom and Dad home?"

"Not yet," Rachel told him over her shoulder. "It's just some friends of your sister's."

I didn't bother to correct her. "Hi, Lewis," I called to the little boy in a friendly voice. "Listen, do you have any idea where your parents went tonight?"

The boy yawned and rubbed his eyes. "Huh?" he said sleepily. "Are they home yet? I want to tell them about Captain America and the evil fish. . . ."

I exchanged a glance with my friends. The little boy was so tired that he wasn't making much sense.

Meanwhile the baby-sitter was frowning at us suspiciously. "Hey," she said. "Why are you asking about Mr. and Mrs. S? I thought you were here to see Diane."

"Diane," Lewis mumbled before any of us could answer. "Diane's not here. She got to go play at the cabin and I didn't."

"Cabin?" I said quickly, my sixth sense suddenly buzzing like crazy. "What cabin, Lewis?"

"Oh, don't pay any attention to him." Rachel waved her hand dismissively. "The kid's been complaining all night because Diane got to go to the family vacation cabin up at Lake Firefly. Got to miss music school for it too."

"Yeah." Lewis sounded grumpy. "But I still had to go to arts and crafts day camp and make stupid rope bracelets."

I took a step forward eagerly. "Tell me more about this cabin, please, Lewis," I said. "Where is it, exactly? Do you know the address, or—"

"Hey!" Rachel interrupted. "If you really *are*

friends with Diane, shouldn't you know all this already? Who are you guys anyway?"

I hesitated. "Okay, we don't really know Diane," I said at last. "But we sort of met her mother this week, and we really need some information—"

"I think you'd better come back when Mr. and Mrs. Sharon are here," the baby-sitter said. With one last crack of her gum, she slammed the door shut in our faces.

I clenched my fists, aggravated at how close we'd come to getting the information we needed. Still, at least now we had a trail to follow.

"Come on," I told my friends, spinning around and hurrying back toward the car. "We're going to Lake Firefly!"

10

A Long Drive

ake Firefly?" Bess caught up with me halfway to the car. "Are you kidding? That's at least a four-hour drive from here!"

I kept walking. "So we'd better get started."

"Wait, Nancy," George added. "Even if Leslie is up there at that cabin with Diane, doesn't that solve the mystery? The two of them must be on a sort of rehearsal retreat, just like Mrs. Sharon told you. They'll probably both be back in plenty of time for their auditions tomorrow morning."

"I'm not so sure about that," I said darkly. "If Leslie went up there of her own free will, why wouldn't she tell her parents? It just doesn't make sense."

I had reached my car by now. Opening the driver's-side door, I slid in and buckled my seat belt. Then I

111

glanced out at my friends, who were still standing on the Sharons' driveway looking uncertain. "Coming?"

"But are you saying you think the Sharons kidnapped Leslie?" Bess asked. "Why would they do that?"

"To make her miss that audition tomorrow," I said. "Don't you get it? Everyone in town thinks Leslie is a shoo-in for that scholarship. I mean, even the CEO of Rackham Industries knows about her! With her out of the picture, Diane Sharon has a much better shot at winning."

George looked troubled. She glanced over her shoulder at the Sharons' house. "Now *you're* the one who's not making sense," she told me. "I mean, look at this house—the Sharons obviously have plenty of money. Why go to all that trouble just to win a scholarship? They could pay Diane's way at the conservatory without it."

"I don't know," I said a bit impatiently. "Maybe they're just greedy, or jealous because Leslie's more talented than their own daughter. Whatever their reason, I intend to make sure they don't get away with it if I can help it. And that means leaving for Lake Firefly—now. If you don't want to come along, I can drop you off at home on my way out of town."

Bess sighed loudly. "All right, all right," she said. "I guess we'd better come along. Right, George?"

"I guess so," George said, sounding a bit disgruntled. "But I get the backseat so I can sleep on the way there."

"No problem," I said, relieved. Despite my bold words, I didn't relish the thought of driving all that way in the middle of the night by myself. "But before you start snoozing, you'd better call our houses so they're not worried about us."

"And tell them what?" George climbed into the backseat and pulled out her cell phone. "That we're driving halfway across the state to some kidnapper's vacation cabin?"

Bess was already strapping herself into the front seat. "Just tell our folks that we're staying over at Nancy's," she suggested. "And tell Nancy's dad and Hannah that she's staying with one of us. That way they won't worry."

George nodded. As I drove off past the quiet, darkened homes of the Sharons' development, she placed the calls. My friends and I were getting a little too old for slumber parties, but we did occasionally sleep over at one another's homes for one reason or another, so nobody questioned her story. I felt a little guilty about the lie, but I figured my father would understand when I explained later. He always does.

Soon we were driving up the entrance ramp and onto the main highway, heading north out of town.

Instead of falling asleep as she'd threatened, George had pulled out her handheld and was busily punching keys. The little machine let out a series of clicks and beeps.

"What are you doing?" Bess asked, turning around in her seat to see. "Playing games?"

"Nope," George responded distractedly. "If we're going all the way up to Lake Firefly, we might as well be prepared. I'm researching the Sharons."

"Good plan," I told her, glad that she seemed at least a little bit more interested in the case. "Let me know if you find out anything good."

George nodded. Several minutes passed in silence, except for the bloops and bleeps of the computer and the sound of soft music from the radio, which Bess had just switched on. Then I heard George let out a low whistle. "Well, this explains a lot," she commented.

I glanced at her in the rearview mirror. "What?" I asked. "What did you find?"

"It seems the Sharons are in debt up to their earlobes," George replied. "All their money is going toward paying for their fancy house, the vacation cabin, and a couple of expensive cars. They really don't have much to spare for stuff like conservatory tuition."

"The conservatory isn't cheap, either," Bess added.

"A few months ago Maggie told Mom and Dad that she wanted to go there instead of to 'real college,' as she called it." She grinned. "Mom and Dad knew she was just looking for an excuse not to study for her math test. So they found out how much the tuition would be, and told her she had to save up at least half if she wanted to go there. That was the end of that."

I chuckled at Bess's story. Her twelve-year-old sister was always coming up with crazy schemes. My smile faded, though, as I thought about what George had discovered. I found myself grimly unsurprised to hear about the Sharons' money problems. Hadn't Dad once told me that most crimes had something to do with money? It was only in the movies that people did desperate things for love or revenge or other reasons. In real life, the almighty dollar was usually the primary motive.

Gripping the steering wheel tighter, I pushed my car right up to the speed limit and held it there. Luckily there wasn't much traffic on the highway at that time of night.

"It's all starting to make sense now," I said. "I just hope we're not too late. If poor Leslie is trapped up there at that cabin, she's probably frantic at the thought that she's going to miss out on something she's worked so hard for. If we want to help her, we can't lose any more time."

"You're not kidding about that," Bess said, squinting at her watch in the dim light. "It's way after eleven. We may already be too late."

"We're not too late," I said with determination. "Not yet. And I'm going to do everything I can to make sure she doesn't miss that audition."

"But what if the Sharons are up there with her?" George asked. "What if they try to stop us from taking Leslie back home?"

Bess glanced over her shoulder at her cousin, looking worried. "You don't think they'd do that, do you?"

"Of course not," I said with more conviction than I felt. "The Sharons are obviously feeling desperate, or they wouldn't try something like this at all. But they're not criminals. They're not going to, you know, *shoot* us or something. We'll just calmly tell them that the game is over, and ask Leslie to come back with us. Once we get her to that audition, Leslie's parents and the police can decide what to do from there."

"I guess." George still sounded a little doubtful. "I mean, I hope you're right. I guess we'll find out in a few hours."

After that, my friends fell silent. George put away her computer, and a few minutes later I heard the sound of soft snores from the backseat. Beside me,

Bess's blue eyes got droopier and droopier until she finally dozed off as well.

Fortunately I was wide awake. I couldn't stop mentally chiding myself for being so focused on one theory that I'd missed the truth. It had been right under my nose all along. The flat, dark, empty highway seemed to stretch on endlessly before me, the yellow center divider lines flashing by in a regular, almost hypnotic rhythm.

I should have suspected something like this as soon as I met Mrs. Sharon. Looking back, it was a little odd how quick she was to start blabbing about Leslie's rehearsal retreat and everything. But at the time, I was still too focused on Morris Granger's possible motives to think about anyone else's. I shook my head in frustration. Now we'd be lucky if we could find Leslie and get back in time.

But exactly how much luck would we need? I ran the numbers in my head. We had left River Heights at around 11 P.M. Lake Firefly was about a four-hour drive from there. That meant that if we didn't run into any trouble, we should arrive in the lakeside town by three o'clock in the morning.

Of course, then we'd have to try to find the Sharons' house. I decided I'd wake George up when we got closer, and see if she could track down the address online. If we could find Leslie and get back on the road right away, we'd be back in River Heights by 7 A.M. That left us time to spare to get Leslie to her 8:15 audition.

After working it out, I smiled. It would be touch and go, but maybe we would be able to pull it off after all.

Just then the car's engine, which had been purring smoothly, let out a disturbing sputter. Then another. A moment later I felt the power in the gas pedal dropping sharply. I barely had time to steer over to the shoulder before the engine cut off entirely.

I gulped, glancing down at the instrument panel. With a sinking feeling in the pit of my stomach, I saw that the gas gauge was resting squarely on *Empty*.

11

Too Late?

A argh!" I cried. I felt like banging my head against the steering wheel. Why hadn't I checked the gas tank before we left River Heights? But I already knew the answer to that. Like so many times before, I'd been too focused on solving the mystery to think about anything else.

"Wha—whu—huh?" Bess snorted sleepily as she opened her eyes and gazed over at me. "What's going on? Are we there yet?"

"Not exactly." I cleared my throat, steeling myself for her reaction. "Um . . . we seem to be out of gas."

Bess smacked herself on the forehead. "Stupid! Stupid!" she cried.

I frowned at her. "You don't have to be insulting," I protested.

"I wasn't talking to you," she said. "I was talking to myself. What's wrong with me? I should know to double-check you on stuff like that by now. It's not like this is the first time something like this has happened. Or the second. Or the forty-third."

By this time George was awake too. She leaned over the back of the seat and just stared at the gas gauge. "Well," she said fuzzily after a long pause. "Isn't this just superfantastic?"

I glanced out the window at the dark, deserted stretch of highway. If there were any houses or other buildings within a couple of miles, we couldn't see them—the moon was behind a bank of clouds, and it was too late for lights to be glowing through windows. I tried to remember the last village or farm we'd passed that was relatively close to the road. As I thought back, I also realized that no cars had passed in either direction for at least ten minutes.

"Someone's got to come by sooner or later," I said.

"I'm sure someone will," Bess responded. "But do we really want to flag down some unknown stranger in the middle of nowhere at this hour?"

I had to admit that she had a point. Bess tends to look on the bright side whenever possible, so when she's worried about something, it usually means there's something to worry about.

George held up her cell phone. "Don't worry," she

said wearily. "I'll see if I can track down the closest garage. Well, the closest garage that's open *all night*."

It took quite a few calls, but George finally managed to get through to an all-night truck stop and convince one of the workers to come to our rescue with a can of gas and directions back to the truck stop. We were on the road again within an hour and a half with a full tank and a new appreciation for Good Samaritans like the truck stop worker. He even refused to take any money for his trouble.

"That guy was sweet, wasn't he?" Bess commented as we pulled away from the truck stop. She waved to the worker who had rescued us as he watched us go. "It was nice of him to help us out like that."

George laughed. "Uh-huh," she said. "I'm sure it didn't hurt that you kept fluttering your eyelashes at him. Good thing you had plenty of time to check your makeup while I was making those calls."

As Bess protested, I laughed—but I wasn't feeling especially cheerful. I was all too aware that we'd lost valuable time. Whatever cushion we'd had was gone; our luck was going to have to hold from now on if we wanted to have any chance of getting Leslie to her audition on time.

I mentioned this to my friends. "So let's try to be prepared," I suggested. "George, can you look up the

Sharons' address at Lake Firefly? That way we can find it on the map and not have to waste any time when we get there."

"Sure," George said. "I should be able to manage finding one simple address sometime in the next two and a half hours."

We drove on in silence broken only by an occasional chirp from George's computer. After a few minutes, though, I heard her let out a frustrated sigh.

"What's wrong?" I asked, peering at her in the rearview mirror.

"It's nothing," she muttered. "I'm just having a little trouble finding any address listings for Lake Firefly, that's all. . . ."

Bess and I exchanged a worried glance. We kept quiet, though, and let George do her thing. Our silence didn't help. Finally George had to admit defeat.

"They must not have any mail service up there," she said with a shrug, sounding irritated. "I mean, it *is* mostly just a vacation town, isn't it?"

"I don't know," I admitted. "I think so. But I've never actually been there myself."

Bess shrugged. "Me either," she said. "I've been to Lake Terrance, though. That's just twenty miles east of Lake Firefly, I think. And it's pretty rustic up there."

"I can't believe they don't list the addresses online,"

George muttered. "Postal service or not, that's just crazy."

Despite my anxious mood, I couldn't help smiling a little at that. George sounded personally insulted by the fact that the information she wanted wasn't on the Internet.

"Well, we'll just have to play it by ear, I guess," I said, still not willing to give up. People had solved mysteries before the Internet ever existed, and we could do it too, if necessary. "We'll just have to check names on mailboxes, go to the local police station— do whatever it takes."

"Right," Bess said. "The local police are going to be thrilled to see us turn up at four in the morning."

I ignored her sarcastic comment. Pressing my foot down on the gas pedal a little harder, I kept my eyes trained on the road.

It was approaching 4:30 A.M. when we finally passed a large, rustic-looking wooden sign reading WELCOME TO LAKE FIREFLY: A PLACE TO UNWIND.

"Okay," I said hopefully as I peered at the buildings visible by the glow of my headlights. "Now let's just hope that this town isn't too big."

Lake Firefly didn't seem like much of a town at first—just a collection of cabins in the woods, lining the single narrow paved road that led straight toward a large lake. My hopes soared. But when I reached an intersection and glanced to either side, my heart sank. More cabins lined both sides of the crossroad that paralleled the shoreline for as far as I could see by the fading beam of my headlights. There were no streetlights and the moon had set, so it was impossible to tell how far the town stretched. Everything was quiet and still at that hour, but the cars in many of the driveways and the occasional porch light indicated that there were plenty of people there enjoying the nice summer weather.

Bess was taking it all in too. "Wow, this place is bigger than it first seemed."

"No kidding," I muttered. How were we ever going to find Leslie in time?

George seemed to be thinking the same thing. "We're never going find her—not at this crazy hour."

"We have to try," I said with determination. "Come on, I'll drive slowly. You guys read the names on the mailboxes."

We wasted the better part of an hour driving around in the dark, peeking at mailboxes. The more time that passed, the more desperate I felt. I couldn't believe it: We were *here,* probably within a few hundred yards of the Sharons' cabin, but we had no way of knowing exactly where it was.

For a while Bess and George had shared my sense of urgency. They'd both rolled down their windows, leaning out and squinting at the faded names and numbers on the mailboxes. George had also spent a while grumbling about those mailboxes—if there was mail delivery after all, she couldn't understand why the addresses weren't listed on the Net. She even pulled out her computer and checked again, with no more luck than she'd had the first time.

Every time we thought we were reaching the edge of town, we rounded a curve in the road or turned a corner and found a new row of cabins in front of us. After a while all conversation in the car faded. I would drive from one house to the next, pause just long enough for Bess and George to check for a mailbox name or other clues, and then move on in silence. Soon we were all yawning almost nonstop, and I was starting to wonder how much longer we could go on before we would have to face defeat and crash somewhere for a while.

As I idled at a stop sign, I checked the clock on the dashboard. It was 5 A.M.

Well, that's that, I thought with resignation. We'd

never be able to make it back by 8:15 A.M., even if we found Leslie that minute.

Still, I didn't want to give up. Not when there was any chance of making this come out right. I decided to drive on, trying to think positive thoughts. Maybe the auditions would run late. Maybe they would let Leslie switch times with someone else. Maybe . . .

My head was spinning, partly from the stress of our search and partly from lack of sleep. When I'd spent a good thirty seconds staring at a brown house with a blue mailbox, trying to remember if we'd already checked this block, I decided that I needed some fresh air.

"I'm going to stop for a sec," I said. "You know—stretch my legs."

Bess mumbled something unintelligible and rested her head on the window ledge. George didn't bother to reply at all.

I pulled to the side of the road—there were no curbs or sidewalks in Lake Firefly, just sandy lawns stretching to meet the blacktop—and cut the engine. Glancing at Bess and George, who were both at least half asleep by then, I climbed out of the car.

My legs felt stiff and a little numb after driving for so many hours without a break. I did a few stretches, breathing in the cool, clean night air, which smelled pleasantly of pine needles and earth. I glanced around at the cabins nearby. One or two of the windows were showing lonely spots of light as dawn approached and the early-rising creatures prepared to meet the coming day. Now that the car motor was off, the buzz of nighttime insects droned lazily around me, and a few birds chirped and whistled. But suddenly I realized that that wasn't all I was hearing. . . .

"Hey!" I blurted out, leaning into the car and poking Bess. "Wake up. I think I know which house we want!"

Bess and George came awake at once. "Huh?" George said. "How? What do you mean?"

"Listen."

They climbed out of the car and stood beside me. After a moment Bess's look of sleepy confusion changed to one of amazement.

"It's a piano!" she cried. "Someone's playing the piano!"

I nodded, grinning. The strains of a familiar classical piece were easy to hear in the early-morning stillness. "Sounds like it's coming from that house," I said, pointing to an attractive cedar-shingled cabin across the road and a few houses down from where we were standing.

"Well, what are we waiting for?" George exclaimed.

Leaving the car where it was, we jogged down the street to the house in question. A light gleamed from one of the front windows. The piano music grew louder as we approached—it was definitely the right house.

"Come on," I told my friends, already marching toward the front door. "Let's do what we came here to do."

I knocked on the door. The piano music stopped instantly, and seconds later the door flew open to reveal a slim, pretty teenage girl with long black cornrows and an anxious look on her face.

"There you are!" Leslie Simmons cried. "I thought you said you'd be here by . . . wait a minute. Who are you?"

"Hi, Leslie," I said with a reassuring smile for the startled girl. "It's me, Nancy Drew, from River Heights. We've met a few times, remember?"

"Oh, of course!" Leslie said, clearly doing her best to regain her composure. "Hello. Did the Sharons send you to pick me up or something? I was expecting them an hour and a half ago. They were supposed to come get me and take me back to town for an audition."

I exchanged a glance with Bess and George. "It's

sort of a long story," I said. "That's the reason we're here."

Leslie looked alarmed. "There wasn't an accident or anything, was there?" she cried, clutching the door anxiously. "Is someone hurt?"

"No, no, nothing like that," I assured her hastily. "Um, did you say that the Sharons were supposed to pick you up?"

Leslie nodded. "Mr. Sharon and I arranged it yesterday. He was supposed to come back up here and get me at three thirty A.M. That way we'd have plenty of time to get back to town before my audition time." She shrugged. "But three thirty came and went, and nobody showed up. And I couldn't call—there's no phone in the cabin."

"Don't you have a cell phone?" George asked.

"No," Leslie said.

Ignoring George's look of amazed disbelief at that bit of information, I focused on Leslie. "Listen," I told her as gently as I could. "We think you've been the victim of some troublemaking. We're here because we don't think Mr. Sharon is coming for you at all— at least not until you've missed your audition. We're pretty sure the Sharons invited you up here for that very reason—because they want to make sure that Diane wins the scholarship."

"No way!" Leslie said immediately. "Diane is one of my best friends. She wouldn't do that to me!"

"Maybe not," Bess said kindly. "But I'm afraid her parents did."

George nodded. "They had it all worked out," she said. "No phone, no way home on your own—they figured you'd be stuck here until they were ready to come and get you."

I shot George a warning look—sometimes she can be a little too blunt—and then gazed sympathetically at Leslie. She looked shocked, confused, and anxious at the same time.

"Come on," I said. "Why don't you grab your stuff and come with us? We can talk about this more in the car."

Leslie nodded. "I'll be right back," she mumbled. A moment later we heard her rustling around in a back room.

George leaned against the door and glanced at her watch. "Well, it's official," she said, keeping her voice low so only Bess and I could hear. "The Sharons' plan worked. There's no way we'll get her back in time."

I checked my own watch, which had stopped. It's an old-fashioned one that used to belong to my mother, and I'm always forgetting to wind it. Grabbing Bess's arm, I checked hers instead. It was ten minutes after five. But I refused to believe that we'd come all this way only to miss out on saving the day by an hour.

"You never know," I said. "It could still work out."

"Come on, Nancy," George said. "How are we supposed to make a four-hour drive in three hours? Even if we *don't* run out of gas this time?"

"Zip it," I hissed at George as Leslie came back into sight with an overstuffed backpack slung over her shoulder. "We're going to do what we can, okay?" I smiled brightly at Leslie as she reached us. "Ready to go?"

"I guess." Leslie closed and locked the cabin door, then followed us to the car.

Dawn was breaking over the lake as I started the engine. My stomach was grumbling, and my eyelids felt like they were lined with wool. It had been a very long night—and it wasn't over yet. Stifling a yawn, I pulled onto the road and headed for the highway.

Bess was sitting in the back with George, while Leslie was in the passenger seat across from me. I glanced over and saw that she was staring blankly out the window. Unlike the rest of us, she didn't look sleepy—just sad and worried. "Can you tell us exactly what happened?" I asked her softly.

She glanced at me. "Sure," she said. The truth of the situation seemed to be sinking in at last. "It was all Mrs. Sharon's idea—the rehearsal retreat up at the cabin, I mean. She said it would give Diane and me a chance to really focus on our music for a few days without any distractions. We didn't want to miss the recital at our camp, but she insisted that the auditions were more important." She shrugged. "I thought she was right, but I still felt bad about leaving Mrs. Diver in the lurch."

"So where did Diane go?" George asked from the backseat. "You said she was up here with you, right?"

"Her dad came to get her yesterday morning," Leslie explained. "She had a dentist appointment back in River Heights. But he said I should stay for one last night, since I'd have a more peaceful night's rest, and more time to practice on their piano—it's a really nice piano." A note of admiration crept into her voice.

"Didn't you think that was sort of strange?" George asked. "Him making this long drive twice in two days, I mean?"

"Of course!" Leslie said. "Diane and I both thought it was totally weird. But he insisted. And I had no reason to think there was anything wrong."

"But what about your parents?" Bess asked. "They're really worried about you."

Leslie turned to stare at her. "What?" she said. "Why would they be worried? They knew where I was."

"I'm afraid they didn't," I told her gently. "They've been frantic. As far as they know, you just disappeared."

Leslie gasped. "I can't believe this!" she exclaimed. "Mr. and Mrs. Sharon told me that my parents knew all about the retreat. They said my parents had thought it was a great idea!"

"Was that why you didn't write much in the note you left?" Bess asked her.

George shot her cousin a scoffing look. "Keep up, Bess," she said. "Isn't it obvious? Leslie didn't write that note. Her folks even said it didn't look like her handwriting, remember?"

"Note?" Leslie sounded confused. "What note?"

We explained it to her. "The Sharons must have planted it at your house somehow," I finished.

She looked shocked. "I can't believe they would do something like that! This is terrible. I can't believe my parents have been worrying about me all this time. . . ."

I felt sorry for her. George offered Leslie her cell

phone so she could call home. Soon Leslie was sob-
bing into it as she explained the whole situation to
her parents.

I clenched the steering wheel and pressed down a
little harder on the gas pedal, more determined than
ever to get her home in time for that audition.

12

Results and Rewards

Despite my good intentions, it was almost 10 A.M. when we drove into River Heights. We'd gotten lost once after leaving the highway for a bathroom break, and then as we neared River Heights we'd been caught in snarled rush-hour traffic. Leslie had called her parents several times to report on our progress, and they had promised to meet us at the conservatory.

They were standing on the sidewalk outside the building when I pulled into the closest parking space. I was so exhausted I barely had the strength to turn the key to cut the engine, but Leslie immediately bounded out of the car and flung herself into her parents' arms.

After a few noisy, confusing moments of happy

reunion, the family pulled apart. "Well?" Leslie asked her parents hopefully.

By that time Bess, George, and I had dragged ourselves out of the car. I waited with bated breath, hoping for some good news.

But it looked like we wouldn't get it. Clay Simmons shook his head sadly. "I'm sorry, sweetie," he told his daughter. "Your mother and I tried every which way to convince them to wait for you. But they insisted that the audition times were final, and that there would be no makeups."

We all went inside the conservatory building, still hoping for some sort of miracle. But we soon learned that the last round of auditions had just ended. The judges were conferring. A few minutes later it was official: The award had been won by a flautist from West Heights.

"At least those rotten cheaters the Sharons didn't win," George muttered with some satisfaction. "Their plan failed."

I was glad about that too, but it didn't make me feel that much better. I could tell that Leslie's family was feeling the same way.

"Oh, well," Leslie said, trying to sound cheerful and failing miserably. "I'm sure there will be other scholarships."

Her mother pulled her into a tight hug. "Don't

worry, sweetheart," she whispered into Leslie's hair. "We'll find some way to pay for your training. I promise."

Leslie looked up at her. "But how?" she asked. "The conservatory is so expensive. . . ."

"I don't know," Heather admitted, glancing at Clay, who was standing helplessly nearby. "I don't know. But we'll figure it out somehow."

I was feeling depressed as we all said our good-byes and prepared to go our separate ways. As I fished the car key out of my pocket, I realized it was now officially my father's birthday.

Oops, I thought, more dejected than ever. So much for finding the perfect gift. I'd be lucky if I could stay awake at his party that night. The very thought made me yawn. Gift or no gift, I needed to get some sleep. I was just too tired to shop. Dad would have to understand.

I invited the Simmonses to the party, and they promised to come. Maybe that would help take their minds off everything, I figured sleepily as Bess, George, and I headed back to my car. Or maybe Dad would be able to help them somehow when he heard what had happened.

"Too bad the Sharons are so deeply in debt," George commented as she strapped herself into the front seat. "Otherwise your dad could help Mr. and

Mrs. Simmons sue them for enough money to pay Leslie's tuition."

I smiled slightly. Obviously she'd been thinking along the same lines as I had. "I thought of that, but I'm not sure it would work," I said. "Leslie's still a minor, but she went up there of her own free will. It would be her word against the Sharons'."

"What if Diane testified for Leslie?" Bess wondered from the backseat.

I shrugged. "A teenager testifying against her parents? I don't know."

We fell silent after that, each of us thinking our own sleepy thoughts as I drove through downtown River Heights. The business day had started, and everywhere we looked people were bustling around looking perfectly normal—and awake. Our long drive up to Lake Firefly already seemed like a strange, hazy dream.

After dropping off my friends at their homes, I headed back to my house. Dad had long since left for work, and Hannah had left a note on the refrigerator saying she was at the supermarket picking up supplies for that night's party. Grateful at not having to explain anything just then, I headed straight upstairs and fell into bed, barely pausing long enough to kick off my shoes.

I was so tired that my head was spinning, making

me feel a little dizzy. Spots floated on the backs of my eyelids, dancing to the tune of the classical piece Leslie had been playing when we found her.

Suddenly my eyes flew open and I sat bolt upright. For the first time in hours, I smiled. I'd just had a perfect idea. Maybe I wasn't able to fix Leslie's problems. But if my latest plan worked out, at least one thing that day wouldn't be a total disaster. I reached for the phone on my bedside table.

I spent most of the day sleeping, awaking a few hours before the party feeling refreshed and optimistic about the evening's festivities. Every time I thought about Leslie's lost scholarship, my mood sank a little; I still wished I could figure out a way to help her. But I was determined not to let such worries spoil my father's special day. I threw myself into the party preparations with all the energy I could muster, setting up tables and chairs near the grill in the backyard and helping Hannah prepare mounds of delicious food.

Bess and George arrived a little early to help out too. Soon the backyard looked festive and beautiful. Party lights blinked from the bushes, and bright bouquets of flowers were everywhere. When Dad arrived home from work, he was amazed.

"Wow," he said, putting an arm around my shoulders

and planting a kiss on top of my head as he looked out the kitchen window at the backyard. "I know you said we were having a little cookout for my birthday. But I wasn't expecting anything like this."

I hugged him. "You deserve it, Dad. Happy birthday."

"Thanks." He grinned. "So what'd you get me?" he asked playfully.

"Now, now," I joked back, waggling a finger at him. "You'll just have to wait to find out."

As he headed upstairs to change clothes, the doorbell rang. "Party's on!" George exclaimed.

A group of neighbors were the first guests to arrive, led by Harold Safer, who had brought some buffalo-milk cheese for the party. Soon Bess and George's parents and siblings turned up, and then Lucia Gonsalvo appeared, bearing a large platter of homemade pasta salad.

Dad came back downstairs to greet others as they appeared. Chief McGinnis came with his wife, and Ned brought his family along. Various clients, friends, and neighbors of Dad's kept arriving until it seemed that half the town was in our backyard.

The party was in full swing when I finally spotted Heather, Clay, and Leslie Simmons walking into our backyard and pausing by the drinks table. Right behind them was Morris Granger.

I hurried to meet them, reaching our guests at the same time as Dad. "Hi." I greeted Leslie and her parents with a wink. "I'm so glad you could make it." I thought Dad might be surprised to see that Leslie was back safe and sound, since I hadn't yet had a chance to fill him in on the conclusion of the mystery. But I quickly realized that Heather and Clay must have called him at his office to give him the news. I only hope they hadn't spilled the beans about anything else. . . .

Next Dad turned to shake Granger's hand. From their hearty greeting, I quickly deduced that Granger was one of Dad's clients. I was a little surprised by that; I'd had no idea they knew each other.

Just then Granger turned to me with a broad smile. "And young Nancy!" he declared, reaching out to pump my hand. "It's delightful to see you again, as well."

"Again?" Dad raised an eyebrow at me quizzically. "I didn't realize you two were acquainted."

I grinned at him sheepishly. "Yes, we met yesterday," I admitted. "It's sort of a long story."

With Morris Granger's help, I quickly filled Dad in. Leslie and her parents listened silently, sipping at sodas, and halfway through the story Bess and George wandered over to join the group.

By the time we finished telling the story, Dad was

shaking his head. "I should have guessed," he said. "Anytime Nancy gets that faraway look in her eyes, it means she's on the trail of another mystery."

Mr. Granger laughed, reaching for a second soda. "Well, she certainly solved the heck out of this one," he said admiringly.

I smiled weakly, exchanging a glance with Bess and George. We'd solved it, all right—but too late to do anything to help Leslie.

"That reminds me," Mr. Granger said. "I suppose this means I owe you that reward, Nancy. Is it all right if I drop off a check tomorrow, or would you like me to wire the money directly into your bank account?"

I gaped at him, not understanding what he was talking about at first. "What?"

"The reward," Mr. Granger repeated. "The ten thousand dollars for the person who tracked down Leslie. That's what I promised, and I never go back on my word." He smiled at me. "Besides, you earned it."

I gulped, finally remembering his offer at the Simmons house the previous night. Ten thousand dollars! Images of all the things I could buy with that kind of money flashed through my head. It was tempting—but I knew what I had to do.

"Well, first of all, if I *did* earn the reward, my

friends earned it right along with me," I said slowly, glancing at Bess and George. "If you'll just let me talk with them for a moment . . ."

The three of us huddled a short distance away. When Bess and George heard what I had in mind, they both quickly nodded, even though I could see that George had been adding up in her mind all the electronic equipment she could buy with her share.

We rejoined the group. "We'd like to thank you very much for your generous offer, Mr. Granger," I said. "But if it's all right with you, we'd like the money to go directly to Leslie to help pay her way at the conservatory next year."

Leslie and her parents gasped. "Oh, Nancy!" Heather Simmons exclaimed. "We can't—we *couldn't* . . ."

"Done!" Granger exclaimed, sounding delighted. He shook my hand, then reached for Bess's and George's as well. "I'll have my accountant make out the check first thing in the morning."

Mr. and Mrs. Simmons were still babbling in protest, while Leslie just looked shocked. Bess smiled at them. "I know it won't pay for the whole thing," she said. "But we hope it will help."

"Oh, it will!" Clay blurted out. "That is, it would . . . that is . . . Are you girls really sure about this?"

It took a few more minutes to convince them that we were, indeed, serious. Finally Heather and Clay accepted the offer gratefully, while Leslie burst into tears and hugged me, Bess, and George.

"I don't know how to thank you," she cried. "This is so amazing! How will I ever repay your kindness?"

I grinned. "Well, I can't speak for these guys," I said, gesturing to Bess and George, "but as for me, you can just consider us even now. After all, I owe you one." I winked at her.

Mr. Granger and Dad looked perplexed, but before they could comment, Leslie turned and hugged Mr. Granger.

When she let him go, her mother stepped forward. "I want to thank you too," she told Granger. "Not just for the money, but for everything you've done in helping to find Leslie. I—I wouldn't have expected that. I think I misjudged you." She cleared her throat. "In fact, you've been so generous to us that I'm *almost* tempted to thank you by not declaring for the mayor's race."

She sounded as if she was only half kidding. Morris Granger immediately shook his head, smiling. "I accept your thanks wholeheartedly," he said, taking Heather's hand. "But don't even joke about withdrawing from the election. I want to be mayor, but I also want the people of River Heights to have a real choice."

Heather smiled back at him. "Okay. But now that I know what a nice man you are, I'm going to feel a little guilty about beating you in November."

"We'll see about that," Granger said with a chuckle. "I *still* look forward to doing my best to humiliate you in the polls!"

Heather Simmons laughed. "Fine. Then I'll continue looking forward to beating you in a landslide." Her face fell. "Oh. That's *if* I get my paperwork in on time. I've been so distracted this week . . ."

Suddenly I remembered that the deadline was the next afternoon. Oh, no! After all that had happened, would Heather miss out on the election?

But once again Morris Granger stepped in, offering to send over someone to help get the paperwork in on time. "In fact, I know just the person," he said. "A bright young intern I just hired yesterday. Very smart young lady."

I exchanged a curious glance with Bess and George. Another hunch had just popped into my mind. But it *couldn't* be. . . .

"An intern?" I spoke up. "Where did you find her?"

Granger shrugged. "My good friend Jack just sent

her to me," he said. "Jack Halloran, that is. He's the head of Rackham Industries, you know. He seemed to think she would be a perfect fit for my office."

He, Dad, and the Simmonses looked slightly confused when Bess, George, and I burst into hysterical laughter.

Luckily, Granger's offer to send his new intern Deirdre Shannon to help Heather Simmons seemed to be a sincere—if misguided—offer, rather than an effort to sabotage her. My friends and I also offered our help, as did Leslie and several other partygoers. Before long it was clear that Heather Simmons was going to have no trouble filing her paperwork in time.

The party continued. A few minutes later Chief McGinnis wandered over as Ned and I were telling Lucia Gonsalvo about Leslie's disappearance and rescue. He listened for a moment or two, looking increasingly disgruntled.

Finally he threw both hands into the air, nearly spilling the drink he was holding. "That's it!" he exclaimed. "I might as well just resign right now—Miss Drew here can just handle all the crimes in River Heights herself. She certainly seems to hear about most of them before I do!" He shook his head, muttering something about newspaper headlines and humiliation.

Lucia smiled soothingly at him. "Don't worry, Chief," she said. "I foresee that this particular case will not make the newspapers."

She winked at me. I realized that it was a pretty safe prediction, psychic powers aside. Now that Heather Simmons was definitely going to run for mayor, she wouldn't want that sort of publicity if she could help it. It would only distract the voters from the real issues of the election. In fact, she and Clay had already decided not to press charges against the Sharons. While my friends and I were a little disappointed at the thought that Mr. and Mrs. Sharon wouldn't be punished for what they'd done, Leslie was relieved. It turned out that poor Diane Sharon had been clueless about her parents' scheming all along, and she felt extremely sorry. Leslie didn't want her friend hurt any more than she already was.

As the chief stomped away, still looking grumpy, I checked my watch. "It's time," I whispered to Ned. Glancing around, I saw that Leslie, Hannah, and Mr. Granger were nowhere in sight.

Excusing myself from Lucia, I hurried over and climbed onto a bench near the barbecue grill. "Pardon me!" I called loudly, clapping my hands for attention. When the partygoers were all looking at me, I continued. "Thanks for coming tonight and helping to celebrate Dad's birthday."

I paused as a few people cheered. Dad grinned as several friends clapped him on the back and cracked jokes about his advancing age.

"Okay," I said. "Now, some of you already know that I had a little trouble shopping for a gift for Dad this year. It's not easy to find something special for a man who already has just about everything. I must admit, I never *did* find anything in any of the stores I went to over the past couple of weeks."

Dad stepped forward, smiling at me. "It's okay, sweetheart," he called out. "Bringing Leslie Simmons home safely and even getting her tuition partially paid at the conservatory is really all the gift I need."

Everyone cheered at that. I blushed, realizing that the entire party must have heard about my adventures already.

"Thanks," I said. "But it's funny you should mention Leslie, Dad. . . . If you all wouldn't mind joining me in the living room, I'd like to present Dad's very special gift."

Murmuring curiously, the crowd followed me into the house through the back door. As Dad entered the living room, he let out a gasp. Several pieces of furniture had been pushed back against the walls, and a grand piano was sitting in their place. Several dozen folding chairs were set up nearby. Hannah and Mr. Granger were standing in front of the piano, grinning.

"You—you got me a piano?" Dad sounded perplexed. "That's incredible, but I don't really play—"

"No, no." I laughed. "It's a rental—Mr. Granger and Hannah helped arrange the whole thing. Come on out, Leslie!"

Leslie Simmons stepped into the room from the hall, dressed in a beautiful, flowing black gown. She was holding a sheaf of sheet music, which she placed on the piano as she sat down at the keyboard.

"This is your gift," I told Dad. "Leslie has agreed to play a short recital for us tonight."

Once again the entire crowd cheered. There was a moment of chaos as everyone searched for a seat on the living-room furniture or the folding chairs. The overflow simply sat on the floor or leaned against the walls.

"Thank you, Nancy!" Dad said, giving me a hug as he took the seat of honor right at the front of the audience. "This is the most fantastic gift I've ever received."

I hugged him back. "All right, everyone," I called

out. "I think we're ready to get started. Enjoy!"

We all settled back to do just that. As the first lovely notes filled the air, I could hardly stop smiling. After all we'd been through in the past few days, this was just about the happiest ending I could imagine.

She's sharp.

She's smart.

She's confident.

She's unstoppable.

And she's on your trail.

MEET THE NEW NANCY DREW

Still sleuthing,

still solving crimes,

but she's got some new tricks up her sleeve!

NANCY DREW

girl detectiv

Have you read all of the Alice Books?

❑ THE AGONY OF ALICE
Atheneum Books for Young Readers
0-689-31143-5
Aladdin Paperbacks 0-689-81672-3

❑ ALICE IN RAPTURE, SORT OF
Atheneum Books for Young Readers
0-689-31466-3
Aladdin Paperbacks 0-689-81687-1

❑ RELUCTANTLY ALICE
Atheneum Books for Young Readers
0-689-31681-X

❑ ALL BUT ALICE
Atheneum Books for Young Readers
0-689-31773-5

❑ ALICE IN APRIL
Atheneum Books for Young Readers
0-689-31805-7

❑ ALICE IN-BETWEEN
Atheneum Books for Young Readers
0-689-31890-0

❑ OUTRAGEOUSLY ALICE
Atheneum Books for Young Readers
0-689-80354-0
Aladdin Paperbacks 0-689-80596-9

❑ ALICE IN LACE
Atheneum Books for Young Readers
0-689-80358-3
Aladdin Paperbacks 0-689-80597-7

❑ ALICE THE BRAVE
Atheneum Books for Young Readers
0-689-80095-9
Aladdin Paperbacks 0-689-80598-5

❑ ACHINGLY ALICE
Atheneum Books for Young Readers
0-698-80533-9
Aladdin Paperbacks 0-689-80595-0
Simon Pulse 0-689-86396-9

❑ ALICE ON THE OUTSIDE
Atheneum Books for Young Readers
0-689-80359-1

❑ GROOMING OF ALICE
Atheneum Books for Young Readers
0-689-82633-8
Simon Pulse 0-689-84618-5

❑ ALICE ALONE
Atheneum Books for Young Readers
0-689-82634-6
Simon Pulse 0-689-85189-8

❑ SIMPLY ALICE
Atheneum Books for Young Readers
0-689-84751-3
Simon Pulse 0-689-85965-1

❑ STARTING WITH ALICE
Atheneum Books for Young Readers
0-689-84395-X

❑ PATIENTLY ALICE
Atheneum Books for Young Readers
0-689-82636-2

❑ ALICE IN BLUNDERLAND
Atheneum Books for Young Readers
0-689-84397-6

Test your detective skills with these spine-tingling Aladdin Mysteries!

The Star-Spangled Secret
By K. M. Kimball

Mystery at Kittiwake Bay
By Joyce Stengel

Scared Stiff
By Willo Davis Roberts

O'Dwyer & Grady
Starring in Acting Innocent
By Eileen Heyes

Ghosts in the Gallery
By Barbara Brooks Wallace

The York Trilogy By Phyllis Reynolds Naylor

Shadows on the Wall

Faces in the Water

Footprints at the Window